"What Do You Think I Am, A Weakling?"

"I think you're adorable," Sam said to Val. "Which I keep telling you, but you refuse to pay any attention. Are you ever going to tell me where you're from?"

"I told you. Poughkeepsie."

"Val, you've told me Poughkeepsie. You've told me Denver. You've told me Boston. How am I going to track you down and marry you when we get back home if you never tell me the truth?"

"I'd tell you the truth but I'm trying to save you from a fate worse than death—involvement with a bad, bad woman like me."

Sam could see that Val was only teasing—trying to give back as good as she got—but his shrewd eyes suddenly rested on her face.

And he could see that she thought she was telling the truth.

Dear Reader,

I hope you're having a happy winter season, and that you're all reading lots of Silhouette Desire books. This month we have an especially wonderful lineup of love stories, guaranteed to take the chill out of the frosty winter air. (For those of you who live in warmer climates, well, you'll just have to get *warmer!*)

Let's start with Jennifer Greene's *Man of the Month, It Had To Be You.* I know many of you like Ms. Greene's work, because you write and tell me so. And I'm sure you'll find this romance—with its very special hero—making its way to your "keeper" shelf.

Next, there's the third book in Lass Small's delightful series about the FABULOUS BROWN BROTHERS. It's called *Beware of Widows* and I know you'll love this story, written in Lass's unique style.

I'm sure you all remember Suzanne Simms's sparkling, sexy "June Groom" title, *Not His Wedding!* Well, now we have *Not Her Wedding!* Don't worry if you haven't read the first book in this duo; *Not Her Wedding!* stands on its own.

December is completed by some great stuff from ever emotional, ever impressive Karen Keast, *The Silence of Angels;* a new offering from one of my favorites, BJ James, *The Man with the Midnight Eyes,* and some fun from Elizabeth Bevarly, *Jake's Christmas.*

Don't miss a single one of these titles! And until next month, Happy Reading.

All the best,
Lucia Macro
Senior Editor

JENNIFER GREENE
IT HAD TO BE YOU

SILHOUETTE *Desire*®

Published by Silhouette Books New York

America's Publisher of Contemporary Romance

SILHOUETTE BOOKS
300 East 42nd St., New York, N.Y. 10017

IT HAD TO BE YOU

ISBN: 0-373-05756-3

First Silhouette Books printing December 1992

Printed in the U.S.A.

JENNIFER GREENE

lives near Lake Michigan with her husband and two children. Before writing full-time, she worked as a personnel manager, teacher and college counselor. Michigan State University honored her as an "outstanding woman graduate" for her work with women on campus.

Ms. Greene has written over thirty-five category romances for which she has won many awards, including the RITA for Best Short Contemporary book from Romance Writers of America and "Best Series Author" from *Romantic Times*.

Prologue

The Persian Gulf

"**H**ey, Valentine. I need a hand."

Val lifted her head over the crate of boxes, then sprinted toward the Red Cross truck backing up to the tent opening. "Medicine?"

"Medicine. Food. Blankets."

"I love you."

Sam climbed out of the truck and slammed the door. "Talk's cheap. Where's my kiss?"

"Still in your dreams, Shepherd."

Sam cuffed her neck and chuckled. Side by side they unloaded the supplies. The wind bit like acid, stinging sand in their faces as they tried to talk. People milled around them, their heads and faces covered to protect against the sandstorm.

Val hadn't bothered with a hat or headgear, simply because she'd discovered that neither helped. Her curly red hair whipped around her cheeks, and her shirt was open at the throat. She'd only been in the Middle East with the Red Cross unit for two weeks, but that was long enough to know the sand was inescapable.

So were exhaustion and sore, aching muscles. Val had been tired before, but never like this. The makeshift camp on the northern Saudi Arabian border was set up to temporarily care for several hundred Iraqi refugees. Several hundred had climbed to a thousand, and they were still pouring in. Val had been putting in nineteen-hour days. So had everyone else. She felt guilty when she slept. So did everyone else.

"Let me handle that, you goose. It has to weigh fifty pounds. What do you think I'm here for?" Sam scolded her.

"What do you think, that I'm a weakling?"

"I think you're adorable. Which I keep telling you, but you refuse to pay any attention. You ever going to tell me where you're from?"

"I told you. Poughkeepsie."

"You told me Poughkeepsie. You told me Denver. You told me Boston. How am I going to track you down to marry you back home if you never tell me the truth?"

"I'd tell you the truth, Shepherd, but I'm trying to save you from a fate worse than death—involvement with a bad, bad woman like me." Val was only teasing—trying to give back as good as she got—but Sam's shrewd dark eyes suddenly rested on her face.

Averting her gaze, she deliberately doubled her speed at unloading the truck. When that job was done, she flew around fetching him a mug of coffee and a plateful of K rations. Typical of Sam, he bullied her into eating something with him. He accused her—without a shred of evidence—of skipping breakfast and forgetting lunch. Which she had.

The food tasted like sawdust, as did most of their dried rations, and was seasoned with more sand than salt. They ate with plates on their laps, using rickety packing crates for chairs. Sam made jokes about the menu and decor. Everyone groused about the primitive living conditions, except for her. But then, everyone else couldn't wait to go home.

Except for her.

When Sam stretched out his long lanky legs, his knee brushed hers. She carefully tucked her knees together, avoiding any second chance of casual contact. Again she felt his gaze shoot to her face.

Val ducked her head and grabbed the empty plates. Shepherd could become a menace to her emotional health—if she let him. She wasn't about to let him. In a million years, Sam would never believe that she was the bad, bad woman she'd claimed. Val wanted it that way. She hadn't told him where she lived because she never wanted him to know.

Back in Chekapee, Florida, she'd left a life in shambles—a broken marriage, mistakes carved in shame, family and friends who'd turned their backs on her. Back home, guilt had preyed on her mind like a festering sore. She'd been sinking under the weight of despair when the Gulf War broke out.

Many of the other Red Cross volunteers were better prepared than she was, but being thousands of miles from home was the best thing that could have happened to her. At home, her problems had seemed insurmountable.

Here, Val mused, they weren't worth diddley squat. She'd seen a baby born under a star-dusted desert sky, a child whose mother didn't even have a swaddling cloth to wrap him in. She'd seen eighteen-year-old boys who shook through the night, too scared to sleep. She'd seen an old man, sightless and crippled and half-starved, emerging from the desert with a girl child carried in his arms. The refugees pouring across the border were all suffering hunger, terror and exhaustion.

Val wasn't sure yet how she was going to find the courage to go home…but she would never, ever in this life again, wallow in her own self-centered problems. People here were desperately fighting for the most basic right to survive. Anything she'd suffered was minuscule in comparison.

Abruptly she felt a big warm hand tuck a strand of hair behind her ear. A thrum of unwanted awareness tangoed through her pulse. When had Sam stood up, moved so close? And there was a devil in his eyes. "Unfortunately, Valentine, I still have miles to go. I'd better be on my way."

She stepped away. "You want some coffee for the road?"

He didn't, claimed he'd just spill it in the truck. "I'll be back in a couple of days. You gonna be good until then? Catch some sleep, not skip any more meals, take care of yourself?"

"You're worse than a mother hen, Shepherd. Don't you ever let up?"

Sam ignored her. She had to listen to several more minutes of his indefatigable orders before he finally strode toward the truck. Val felt a wistful catch in her heart as she watched him vault into the driver's seat.

She'd never known what to make of Carson Samuel Shepherd. He was the first person she'd met when she'd stepped off the plane with a cargo of other Red Cross recruits. Sam had been their transport, but he hadn't adopted the other volunteers. Just her.

He was taller than six feet, built lanky and lean and too handsome for his own good. He said he was a pilot at home, and that his home was Chicago. How he came to be a Red Cross volunteer, she had no idea. Sam could charm the life story out of a nun who'd taken a vow of silence, but he neglected to mention anything about himself. She knew little about him except that he had a shock of thick brown hair, a smart-ass grin, and far too perceptive caramel-brown eyes.

He'd nicknamed her "Valentine" on sight, which had totally annoyed her. Cute nicknames weren't her style. She'd come to the Gulf with a heart heavier than lead. She'd wanted to help; she'd needed to work, and more than anything in life, she'd wanted to be left completely alone. Sam had no idea what troubles she was carrying. He couldn't. Yet from the start, he'd cut her from the pack and—damn him—taken care of her. He checked on her whenever he brought supplies, teased her until she inevitably laughed, and watched out for her with the zealousness of a protective older brother. Nothing she said shut him up. Nothing she did discouraged him. She'd never met a more aggravating man.

Or a better one.

His truck engine started with wheezing reluctance. Probably the sand had got into it, too. She heard him pop the hand brake, then heard her own voice call, "Sam!"

She suspected he couldn't hear over the roar of the tubercular engine—and hoped he hadn't. The impulse to call him back had been foolish and impulsive. When he stopped and stuck his shaggy head out the window, though, that first foolish impulse was followed by another. She walked toward the truck window with her hands jammed tight in her pants pockets.

"You got a lot of nerve, trying to leave without my kiss, Shepherd."

"I beg your pardon?"

He'd never meant his teasing. Val knew that, sensed it the way any woman sensed when a man was seriously interested or just flirting. Sam thought of her like a sister.

She thought of him as a friend, and the need suddenly pressed on her heart to express how much he'd meant to her. She swung up onto the driver's doorstep and balanced a hand on the window ledge. "Don't try to get out of it," she said darkly. "You've been good to me, and you know it, and I don't have time to fool around arguing with you. Just gimme my kiss."

She thought he'd grin. He didn't. She thought he'd make some suggestive comment. He didn't do that, either. Long before she had the good sense to change her mind and back down, his arm shot out the window and latched around her neck. He tilted his head and his mouth came down at a slant on hers.

She expected a sassy smack...but again she was terribly wrong. Sand, sun, wind blurred in her vision. For a long moment, there was only Sam. He held her still, so still that the shape of his hand branded the back of her neck. His lips were warm, wooing warm, capturing hers with a pirate's greed and a man's possessiveness. The kiss packed more than camaraderie, more than teasing, more than the kindness she'd come to know in him. It dived as deep as a submarine into the velvet dark emotions she kept guarded and private, touched off land mines of sensitivity . . . and terrified her.

He didn't kiss like a friend. He kissed like a lover. Val didn't know he felt that way, didn't want him to feel that way, didn't want to feel the stunned impact of heat shimmering clear to her toes. When he finally lifted his head and she saw the look in his eyes, she gulped.

Then he smiled. "You didn't realize," he murmured.

"Realize what?"

"That I always meant it. When this is all over—when we're all home again—I'm going to find you, Valentine."

"No—"

"Yeah, I am. And that's a promise."

"*No*, Sam—"

But he didn't listen—the exasperating man *never* listened—and when he drove off, Val just stood there, feeling unnerved and bemused and oddly shivery.

Slowly, though, she dragged a hand through her hair and calmed down. Everything would be all right. She would make it all right the next time she saw him, by being carefully friendly but distant. They wouldn't be in the Gulf that much longer, and she wouldn't make the mistake of inviting any more kisses. Or any other kind of closeness.

Sam didn't know her, not really. And even if he'd meant that crazy promise, he had no way to keep it. Val had never told him where she lived and never would.

He had no possible way to find her back home.

One

___

Sam stepped out of the airplane rolling his shoulders. It had been a long flight from Chicago to Chekapee, Florida. His neck muscles were cramped and his temper as restless as a tomcat in a full moon.

It had taken months to track down Val this far. Then more time, waiting for a stretch when his brother was free to take over the business for him. Now he was within miles of seeing her. Anticipation triggered his pulse. So did determination.

From the sky, her little burg of a town had appeared like the bull's-eye of a target—just a small dot, circled by sweeping acres of citrus groves in every direction. The ocean, he'd noted, was only a spit of a drive to the east.

There wasn't much else he could learn about where she lived from the air. Obviously he'd expected it to be warmer here than in Chicago. At home, on the first of

November, the nights were frosting and the last leaves spitting off the trees. Here, the radar forecast had claimed unseasonable temperatures, but he truly hadn't expected an afternoon of broiling heat. Blistering hot sunshine poured onto his back as he crossed the tarmac to the tiny control tower.

He checked in and arranged for maintenance and space for his plane. He had to chitchat long enough to make sure he was dealing with good people, but as quickly as he could escape, he asked for directions to a car rental.

Apparently there was only one, and, typical of small towns, it was located at the end of the air strip. The owner was a wizened old man with a melon for a belly, who apparently hadn't seen a customer all day. There were only six cars in the lot. The gregarious old guy wanted to discuss their individual merits in detail.

Sam just wanted wheels—fast—and the fastest set of wheels on the lot was a white convertible Mustang. Yet even after he'd shuffled through the paperwork and paid in plastic, the owner trailed him back into the baking-hot sun.

"If you need it longer than a week, now, I'll make you a good rate. You just give me a call—"

"Okay. Thanks."

"We don't get many out-of-town visitors, but you'll find it's a nice friendly town. Nothing like a big city. You need any help around here, and all you have to do is give a shout—ten people'll come running...."

The old man was obviously lonely. Sam couldn't just shut him off, but his mind was spinning in other directions. He stowed his tote and jacket and started peeling down car windows. There was no escaping the soul-baking sun, and the sultry humidity was impossible to ignore. *So you're used to living in heat, Valentine?*

Not to worry. I'm about to give you as much heat as you could possibly handle.

"I'll give you my card. Like I said, my name's Gatchell. Fred Gatchell. If you have any trouble with the car..."

"I'm sure it'll be fine," Sam said, and took the card as he climbed in. The seat was red leather and stuck promptly to his spine, but the engine started with an even purr and a promise of power. The old man could have taken the hint that he wanted to be on his way.

But no. He kept talking, sweat pouring off his wrinkled brow, his friendliness as untiring as his big jowly smile.

Sam popped on a pair of shades. There was only one smile he wanted to see. It wasn't Fred's.

He'd never chased a woman before. Never had to. He'd certainly never pictured himself pursuing a woman cross-country to arrive unannounced and uninvited on her doorstep, and handling this first meeting with Valentine was going to be unquestionably tricky. She'd told him to forget her after the Gulf. She'd explained that any feelings they'd developed for each other were only temporary. She'd explained that many strangers formed an artificial bond when they were thousands of miles from home. She'd explained that they were living under constantly stressful conditions. She'd had a dozen earnest, honest reasons why it was best to say goodbye.

Val gave excellent lectures. Sam had heard them all, several times. But Valentine had never kissed him as if she meant goodbye. She'd kissed him every time as though she couldn't bear to let him go.

A vision of a cherry-soft mouth was branded in his memory. Even on her tiptoes, she only came up to his nose, and in his mind's picture her mouth was small, damp from his kisses, trembling from his kisses. Her lips were parted to gulp in air and showed a peek of pearl-white teeth. She had a tiny crack on her right eye tooth. And a delectable freckle on the swell of her left breast. Her hair was Irish-setter red, curly, and she wore it all pinned up in a proper little mop, but he'd seen it undone. Undone, her hair cascaded almost to her breasts, its texture thick and springy and prone to tangle.

His hands had been good and tangled in her hair more than once. When Val forgot to be careful, when she got confused and started slurring all the incredibly silly reasons why they could never be involved, when that hair of hers started tumbling down... Valentine was downright dangerous. Wild, as he'd only dreamed a woman could be wild for him. Hungry, as if she'd die if he quit touching her. And vulnerable. So damned vulnerable that she'd captured his heart.

A thousand times in the past months, Sam wished he'd made love with her. Unfortunately, no one had a tent to themselves in the Gulf. There were always people and needs and guaranteed interruptions. The only privacy he could steal were a few rare moments on the dusty seat of a truck in the godforsaken desert, and to take her under those circumstances—it wasn't right. Not for Val.

Valentine had never told him what was wrong. But something was. The first time they met, he saw the haunted strain in her soft hazel eyes. In the Gulf everyone was working double shifts, but Val was worse, still on her feet when she couldn't see straight, never taking a break, forgetting to eat. She made everyone else laugh, because she had a sneaky sense of humor and a way of lifting everyone's spirits. But caught alone, and her slim shoulders would be drooping. Left alone, and she'd have driven herself beyond exhaustion.

Sam hadn't left her alone, but he couldn't force her to talk. Valentine had a teensy streak of lioness about protecting other people. She was also bullheaded. There was no way that his tenaciously stubborn redhead could be coaxed, threatened or bribed into drawing anyone else into her problems.

Sam knew about problems. There was a block of his life he still didn't remember—the hellish years around eighteen. Idealists claimed no problem was insolvable, but that was crap. Life slammed everyone against a wall at one time or another. Even good people made bad choices, got in over their heads.

Sam would have steered clear if Val had shut him down, told him no. She'd never told him no. There was a world of difference between a woman who wasn't interested and a woman who was scared, which was how Sam had justified searching for her all these months. If Val honestly didn't want him, he'd have to take that lump.

But if she was in over her head—that was a horse of a different color.

He'd tried to forget her. No go. She was under his skin like a burr, had claimed a corner of his heart that no other woman had touched. Maybe he'd traveled all these miles just to get slammed in the teeth with rejections, but there was no way to know if she needed help—or how she really felt about him—without seeing her again.

He revved the engine and pushed the gearshift into reverse. Ignoring the subtle message, the old man chattered on, his monologue focused now on the brilliance of his three grandchildren. Sam waved a hand. "Fred?" He didn't want to be cruel to the lonely old geezer, but Val was *here,* somewhere in this town, and his storehouse of patience was dwindling fast. "Do you know where Sungrove Lane is?"

Fred's face immediately brightened. "Shore do, shore do. You take Center straight out two miles. See, there's town. Second stoplight is River, hang a right. Sungrove's in a little cul-de-sac, quiet little street, real pretty. Know everyone on the whole block."

"Then you know Valentine?" Sam immediately corrected himself. "Valerie. Valerie Shroeder?"

Pale blue eyes squinted at him, their warmth suddenly turning cool. Fred Gatchell straightened his considerable girth. "That's why you're in town? To find *her?*" He clicked his teeth. "I took one look at you and figured you were a man with some sense."

"Excuse me?"

The old man stuck out his chin. "It's nothing to me. I'm not one to talk. But Shroeder's been a respected name in this town for generations—with one exception. I ain't saying who 'cause it's none of my affair. You'll find out on your own."

Without another word, he turned and hiked into his air-conditioned hut of an office. Sam stared at his retreating form for several seconds, then shook his head and steered for the road.

Fred obviously had an axe to grind, but he must have confused someone else with Val. The vagaries of an old man's mind were Sam's last concern. He concentrated on directions. Or he tried to.

He found Center Street. He found the two-street business district on River Street but no cul-de-sac name Sungrove. His first circle around town gave him the look of where Val lived. Chekapee was old, sun bleached, whitewashed and carrying an old Spanish flavor—many buildings were stucco, with arches and tiled patios. He liked it. It looked as if the main drag had suffered through a recession and come back. Storefronts had been spiffed up, palms planted in pots and wrought-iron benches lined the sidewalks. There was an old-fashioned town square with a clock tower.

He counted a motel, a hardware, grocer, three gas stations, two bars, three churches, several hair dressers, two restaurants—and a Chinese take-out—a bookstore, craft shop, a couple of clothing stores. The bank had the Shroeder name on it, so did a side street. Val's family? At the edge of town was an agricultural implement dealer and a huge packing house—citrus was obviously the major industry.

It all interested Sam the first time around, and even the second, but exasperation snagged his attention when he made a U-turn for the third time. It was a thriving little town, but hardly a metropolis. Sungrove had to be on the Monopoly board; he just couldn't find it.

At the nearest gas station, the attendant came out to help him—a woman, broad faced and broad beamed, wiping the grease from her hands with an old rag. "There's no sign for Sungrove, that's your problem, honey. You'll be okay. Go a quarter mile, take the first road—that's Sungrove. There's a hydrant at the corner, two cypress trees in old man Richards' yard.

His house is pink, not likely you'll miss it. Richards is a Baptist," she said, as if that explained why the man had painted his house pink.

She patted Sam's wrist, as familiar and friendly as if he were her long-lost nephew. Sam suspected that she was related to Fred, either that, or gregarious friendliness was contagious in Chekapee. But once she mentioned the weather and her allergies, she seemed to peter out of chitchat. "Well, you have any trouble, you just come back, you hear? And who are you looking for on Sungrove? I know just about everybody—"

"Valerie Schroeder."

She straightened as if a sword had just shot up her spine. *"Her!"*

Sam could have sworn that he'd just heard another voice hiss that single word—*her*—with the same sucked-lemon expression. Before he could reply, she leaned forward with a shake of her head.

"I don't mind anybody's business, mind you, but it's obvious that you're new in town. Henry and me had twenty thousand put away, nickel and dimed, saved all our lives to get a little ahead. It's all gone now. Every penny. I'm not saying who's responsible—I'm not one to tell tales—but if I were you, I'd watch my p's and q's around some people." She rapped the window ledge with her knuckles and stood straight. "You get my drift?"

She stalked off through the open doors of the station garage and disappeared, leaving Sam staring in blank bewilderment. First Fred, now her—both had reacted to Val's name as if they'd been exposed to poison. Maybe it was a heat-born virus. Maybe the whole town was crazy.

Obviously they had Val confused with someone else.

He put the car in gear. Within minutes he found the signless street with the hydrant and pink house on the corner, and at the end of the circular cul-de-sac, Val's place.

He parked and climbed out. There was no garage, only an open carport—empty. Next to the carport was a tiny white house with dark red shutters, closed up against the heat. An air conditioner drummed in the background, but there wasn't a sign of life or movement. He glanced at his watch. It was just after five. Too early to expect her home if she was working.

But not by much. He raked a hand through his hair, then stuck his hands into his jeans pockets, figuring that he'd wander around the place and unobtrusively explore.

Wrong. He hadn't stepped two feet from his car when the front door was yanked wide open and a boy stepped out. The urchin was eight or nine, and looked like a natural from the inner-city streets of Chicago. His skin was darker than mahogany, his eyes old and defiant, his shirt and shorts ragged and too big for his bony frame. He was homely as sin. He was also carrying a baseball bat. "Hey. This is private property, mister."

"I know. I'm looking for Val Shroeder."

"Yeah? Well, what you want with Val?"

Sam thought it had been a long day and it seemed to be getting longer. The boy was thumping the edge of the bat in his palm in a swaggering effort to look threatening. The bat was nearly bigger than he was. "I'm a friend of Val's. I came to see her."

"So you say. What's your name?"

"Sam Shepherd," he responded patiently.

"Never heard of you," the boy said belligerently.

"Well, I've never heard of you either." Sam tried to keep the dry humor out of his voice. "What's your name?"

"Lincoln."

"And you're obviously a friend of Val's?"

"Her *best* friend. I house-sit her place after school. That means I make sure nobody gets in. It's my job to protect everything." He added meaningfully, "And I make sure nobody hurts her. We stick together, Val and me."

"I see." Sam took another look at his dare-the-world eyes. Even without knowing the child's story, the miniature delinquent was the first thing that made sense since he'd arrived in town. In the Gulf, too, Val had been a sucker for every waif that came along. "I'm glad she has you to protect her."

"People in trouble gotta stick together," Lincoln said sagely. He thumped the bat again. "You better go now."

"I don't suppose it would be all right if I waited for her." Sam glanced at the bat. "I mean, wait outside. I wasn't going to ask you if I could come in."

"You can't come in and you can't stay out, and it wouldn't make any difference anyway because she won't be home until late tonight. Jonesey was sick, so there was nobody else but her at the store."

"The store . . ." Sam echoed carefully.

"The bookstore." Lincoln was clearly impatient. "Where else would she be?"

"Nowhere else," Sam murmured. Seconds later he was back on River Street, thankful that he wasn't dependent on pumping any more information from her bat-carrying protector. He'd spun around town enough times to know there was only one bookstore and exactly where it was.

A few storefronts were empty, but most of River Street was bustling traffic near the dinner hour. The only spare parking spaces were in front of the bookstore, which struck Sam as odd. He parked and climbed back out in the sweltering heat, thinking that a few too many things were odd in this town. His pulse was edgy, his heart thudding an unsettled beat. The boy at her house hadn't really disturbed him; neither had his quick encounters with the two townspeople. It was just that he wanted to see Val.

He needed to see Val.

The sign in the casement window said Book Nook and had a tasteful display of books on red velvet. When he stepped in, a bell jangled, and he was immediately conscious of a million smells. Soft smells, like lily of the valley and moss rose and maybe, somewhere, vanilla. It took a second for his eyes to adjust from the harsh sunlight, and he just stood there.

The smells were coming from antique wooden barrels, some piled with candles, some with fresh potpourri. In a corner were two chairs—huge old-fashioned morris chairs—set up as a reading niche with pitchers of coffee and iced tea on the table behind. Another corner was organized for children, with kid-sized overstuffed chairs and miniature ottomans and a display of books within reach. Scented herbs hung from the beams; the drapes were red and tied back with sashes. Books were everywhere, piled and clustered and stashed in long rows by subject, but it wasn't like being in a store. It was like being in a soothing, quiet, softly lit haven away from the cares of the world.

Only Sam wasn't soothed. His pulse was drumming an even more unsettled rhythm. The place was quieter than a tomb. There wasn't a single customer in the store. There wasn't even a footprint in the fresh-vacuumed carpet.

And there was no sight or sound of Val.

Val thought she heard the bells jangle, but she waited a second and heard nothing else. It had to be her imagination, she thought.

That conclusion was easy to come by. The only customers she'd had all day—beyond some giggling teenagers and incidental strangers—had been in her imagination.

Tucking a pen behind her ear, Val started punching calculator buttons again. The store had two spare rooms, one a bathroom and the other a closet. Her office was the closet. It held a desk, a chair, a filing cabinet and a phone, which all fit in as long as she didn't try to turn around. She'd been cooped up here for the past three hours. Her eyes were burning and her nerves were frayed.

She punched the Total button. Unfortunately the calculator beast produced the identical figures that it had the last time.

She was going under. Not a little under. *Big* under, down-the-drain bankrupt, wiped-out broke. She had twelve thousand dollars left from her grandfather's trust. Assuming she had no massive increase in customers, and she had no reason to believe that would happen, she could conceivably stay afloat for another month. Not much more. The mortgage payments on the house and store, two electric bills, two phones, car fuel, food... She could give up the house, of course. Set up a cot in the back of the store. Stop eating.

Potentially she could last two more months that way, possibly three. Of course she'd be dead from starvation.

But that was a hell of a lot less humiliating than bankruptcy.

Annoying her no end, she felt the sting of tears in her eyes. Snapping off the calculator, she muttered one of those crude four-letter words that a lady never said, especially if that lady was a Shroeder with generations of aristocratic manners and traditions to uphold. Val threw the pen onto the desk and belted it out again.

From the day she was born, her mother had warned her that cussing had dire consequences. Until Val was eleven, she'd envisioned lightning bolts, rivers swallowing her up, the Reverend Miller stopping by the house. She was twenty-eight now. Long past the age where she even remembered her mother's threats, but she was briefly tempted to believe in them again. There was no other explanation for the apparition suddenly standing in her doorway.

The Gulf conflict was over, the United States long since back to normal. Shepherd had had ample time to come home, charm a good woman and be married to her by now. Val had told him to do just that, had vociferously ordered him to forget her.

But the vision in the doorway looked terrifyingly like Sam. The electricity in the air even *felt* like Sam. The ghost had his same crooked smile, the same sweep of thick caramel-brown hair, the same devil in his eyes. Sam wore his jeans low slung like that, not tight, but curving easy over long lanky legs and a flat behind.

The black T-shirt showed off his muscular arms, his broad chest, and contrasted skin burned gold by the sun.

Wicked. Sam had that same wicked look. A slow grin, full of hell, a land mine of sexuality glinting in his eyes, angular features that he knew *damned* well were good-looking and a chin that should have warned a woman. It was a square chin, a stubborn chin, a trust-me-it'll-be-easier-if-we-do-this-my-way chin.

Val *knew* that chin. In the Gulf, when there was no time to be involved, when she couldn't be involved, when she was painstakingly careful to avoid closeness with anyone, Shepherd had submarined her. To everyone else, Sam was nice. To everyone else, Sam was kind. No one but her had any idea how single-minded and obstinate and dangerous he was.

The vision in the doorway, of course, had to be a ghost. Sam couldn't be there.

Val could face starvation. She could face bankruptcy. But she couldn't—*Please God, don't ask this of me*—face Carson Sam Shepherd again.

The ghost cocked a leg forward and leaned a shoulder against her door. And then said, slow and lazy, "Hi, Valentine."

Two

"Usually I have a million customers. It's just slow on Thursday nights."

"Business pretty good, hmm?"

Val nodded. "You wouldn't believe! In a town this size, a bookstore is really a community resource. There isn't a library for thirty miles, so where else could people go for books? And I know everyone. Everything in stock is geared toward someone's special interest, whether it's agricultural or new-age or sci-fi. That's why the store has done so well."

Sam topped off the wine in her glass. "So how'd you get into it?"

"A woman named Marie Lansdowne owned the store until she retired. When I came back from the Gulf, it was on the market. I had a trust from my grandfather—not a fortune, but enough capital to get started. I didn't know much, but I did have a business

degree and I knew the store—I'd worked here as a
teenager. And it was one of the most successful busi-
nesses in town. All I had to do was follow Marie's
lead.''

''Yeah?''

''Originally the place looked pretty ratty. Marie
never got around to fixing it up. Bare-bone floors,
metal shelves . . .''

''You fixed it up nice.''

''I just wanted it . . . warmer. More inviting. A place
where you wanted to walk in because it made you feel
good. And it's done so well I can hardly believe it.''

''Thriving, hmm?''

''I'm raking in cash hand over fist,'' she confided.

And cats flew, Sam thought.

Two hours before, he'd brought in dinner. The
white cartons of Chinese take-out were still spread out,
picnic fashion, between the bookshelves at the back of
her store. The same restaurant that supplied the food
had kindly provided him with two plastic wineglasses
and a long-stemmed bottle of dark red burgundy.

Val had only nibbled on the food, but she was doing a fine job of single-handedly polishing off the
bottle, thanks to his sleight of hand and sneakiness.

Sam had never envisioned himself getting a woman
drunk. Late in high school, after losing both parents,
he'd done a damn good job of trying to drown himself in alcohol. He'd wasted two years of his life in that
abyss. His brother, Cole, had helped him climb out of
the mess. Sam had long put his life back together, but
the experience had left him with a wariness of anything to do with drinking. From his ethical frame-
work, any man who'd force wine on a woman for
manipulative purposes was lower than a frog turd.

When Val ducked her head to stash their debris in the tall white bags, he refilled her glass to the brim.

There was a time for ethics.

And a time when a man did what a man had to do.

Val lifted her head and smiled brilliantly. Then hiccuped. "Heavens, excuse me." She blinked in surprise and then reached for the glass. Several gulps cured her hiccups. He helped by pouring her a little more wine. "I need to close up."

"You already did," he reminded her gently. "The shades are down, the door's locked. Relax. Finish your wine. And tell me some more about what you've been up to."

She shook her head. "You don't want to hear any more about me. I've been talking too much."

She'd been talking like a bubbling fountain, but Sam hadn't heard anything truthful so far.

Hours before, when he'd caught her bellowing swear words in the back office, she'd been primly dressed in a long slim skirt, matching navy heels and a stiff white blouse. At the moment she was sprawled on the carpet, with her spine supported against the Self-Help bookshelves and a leg tucked under her. The high heels had disappeared. The navy skirt was peeled up over one thigh. The blouse was open at the throat by three buttons—Val was not used to the heat of drinking—and hairpins continued to pop free from her hair. Initially the russet-red mane had been controlled in a feminine twist at her nape. Now tendrils curled damply around the shell of her ears and a lopsided coil was snaking down her throat.

She looked shnozzled. Which was infinitely better than how she'd looked when he first saw her. In that pip-squeak-sized office, her expression had been panic when she recognized him. Sheer, straight, undisguised panic. The flush climbing her cheeks was as scarlet as shame.

He'd expected surprise. He'd geared himself up for rejection. But the look of shame and guilt made no sense, because Valentine hadn't done a damn thing with him that she needed to be ashamed of.

He only wished she had.

"So, tell me some more about how the store is doing."

"I have."

"You told me how great everything was, but you must have run into a glitch or two. Running any small business is a headache."

"Not this one. Everything's been wonderful. I told you—"

"Yeah. I heard what you told me." His voice was soft. There hadn't been a single customer since he walked in, and when she'd locked up the big old-fashioned cash register, he'd caught a look at the till. Valentine seemed determined that he believe she was happy and healthy in her role as bookstore tycoon. There wasn't enough cash in that till to buy beans.

God knows why he had to be attracted to a woman with more pride than sense. She wasn't even beautiful. How could a squirt of a woman be beautiful? The turned-up nose, the too-small red mouth, the fringe of pale lashes...none of it added up to classically pretty. She wore a padded bra, barely had hips. Every man wasn't going to find her sexy.

From the beginning, though, she had more allure than a siren for him. Looks were no measure of a woman. Sexiness was in the eyes, in the way a woman moved, in her style, in the way she related to a man.

On a sexual-attraction scale of one to ten, Sam rated her 175. Even schnozzled. Even when her face was white with fatigue, even when there were huge lavender shadows under her eyes. Even when she was obviously very, very worried about what on earth she was going to do with him.

"Shepherd?"

"Hmm?"

"You can't . . . stay."

"Okay."

"Even if I wanted you to . . . you can't stay."

"Okay."

"If you came here thinking I could . . . thinking we could . . ." She shook her head dizzily, causing the final waterloo of her proper hairstyle. Coils of rowdy rust-and-cinnamon curls tumbled down her shoulders and back. She was too worried to notice.

"Take it easy, Valentine. I just stopped to see you, nothing more, no heavy expectations implied." Sam easily justified the blatant lie. It immediately eased the fever-bright anxiety in her soft hazel eyes. "Nothing wrong with two old friends having dinner, is there?"

"No, of course not."

"We *were* friends, the last I knew . . ." He leaned forward with his most reassuring, trustworthy smile. Never breaking eye contact with Val, he upended the last of the wine bottle into her glass. "And it's hard to beat an old friend for a listening ear. Nothing's going further than the two of us, you know that, don't you? And I can see how terrific everything's going for you, but there must be something. Some teensy thing that maybe you'd like to unload."

Even a rock as tough as Gibraltar eventually suffered the effects of erosion. He'd fed her nearly enough wine to erode the Grand Canyon, but until that instant, he hadn't seen any effect. Finally the starch was sneaking out of her shoulders. And when she met his eyes, for the first time he caught a glimpse of a very fragile, very wounded soul. "I don't want anyone worried about me," she said firmly.

"Worried? Who said anything about being worried?" He wanted to haul her onto his lap and kiss her until that terrible look in her eyes went away. Even in the Gulf, he'd known she had trouble. He was expecting anything from a range of awkward ex-lovers to some dark traumatic secret in her family closet. Whatever the problem was, he didn't give a damn, then or now. Sam had made too many mistakes to judge anything Val could possibly have done. Unfortunately, he couldn't prove that to her until he got her to talk. "I'm not *worried* about you. It's obvious you're doing just fine. But for heavens' sakes, that doesn't mean you couldn't have an occasional problem."

"Well, it's possible," she admitted, "that I may have slightly exaggerated the success of the store."

"Yeah?" He feigned surprise, but he already knew about the salad course. He wanted to hear about the meat and potatoes.

"I'm not really doing that well, but there's a good reason for that. A temporary circumstance. Right now everyone . . . the whole town . . . thinks I'm a thief."

Sam blinked. *This* was her big dark secret? "Trust me, honey, the whole town can't be that stupid."

"They're not stupid. They're hurt and angry. And broke." Val closed her eyes, and out it came like the gush of a well. "Chekapee's economy doesn't run to millionaires, Sam. They're just regular people who work very hard to put something away. Most of them put their extra savings in the local bank. And it's gone. The bank was ripped off—an inside job—by an embezzling swindler of a thief.'' Val sighed. ''They caught the jerk. He's behind bars. Some of the money was recovered, but he'd invested quite a bit of it straight down the tubes. So the bottom line is that almost everyone was hurt.''

Sam didn't catch every word—she was starting to slur any word over two syllables—but he understood enough to realize that her story was real and no wine-induced invention. ''That's rough,'' he said, ''but I don't see what it has to do with you.''

Val said dryly, ''I was married to the jerk.''

''Pardon?''

''Married. Four years. To the thief who ripped off the whole town.''

''Whoops.''

''It was a fairly major whoops, Sam.''

''I imagine it was.'' He caught the glass of wine a second before it toppled. Valentine seemed to discover the sudden need to lie down. Leaning over, he checked her eyes. Although the pupils were definitely glassy, no question she was still wide-awake.

''It was the Shroeder bank that he ripped off. Shroeder—as in my family. For generations around here, Shroeders have been pillars of the community, upstanding citizens, denizens of respectability and tradition.'' She had to roll her tongue around ''denizens'' three times before it came out clearly. ''There was never a blot on their copybook. Until me.''

''Is the divorce final?''

''Divorce?''

''Between you and the jerk?''

Her forehead pinched into a puckish frown. "Of course the divorce is final. I kissed you in the Gulf. More than kissed you. Don't you remember? You think I would have behaved like that if I were still married? Try and pay attention to what matters, Sam."

"I was," Sam murmured. Her hair looked like tangled red silk against the nubby carpet, and her skirt had slid halfway up her slim, white thighs. She'd crossed her legs. Her right ankle was making concentric circles in the air. Exotic, erotic circles.

She lifted a hand expressively. "I was responsible for getting Ron hired at the bank. Meaning that I badgered my dad into giving him a job. Which everyone in town knows."

"Valentine, no one in his right mind would honestly believe that you conspired with a thief."

"I didn't. But when you're married for four years to someone, you're supposed to know them. They all believe I knew what Ron was doing. I *didn't*. But their money's gone and they're mad and you might as well hear the worst. I never exactly fit in the respectable Shroeder niche even before Ron."

"No?"

"No." Her right foot was still tap-dancing in mid-air. "You know how teenagers dare each other to do stupid things? Like stealing a stop sign, or teepeeing your neighbor's bushes on Halloween?" She said morosely, "Only being a Shroeder, I never got the little dares. I had to teepee the *mayor's* bushes. And got caught stealing the license plate off the *sheriff's* car. The chemistry lab was different. I never meant to start that fire. And it was simply an accident that I drove my dad's white convertible into Susan Simpson's swimming pool—there was something wrong with the brakes, there really was—but by then, I'd sort of built up a small reputation for being a..." She hesitated, but the word wouldn't come to her.

"Hellion?" Sam helpfully supplied.

She blinked at him owlishly. "You're smiling," she accused him.

"That's not a smile, it's a tic. Sometimes I can't control it. Believe me, I'm taking this all very seriously."

"I reformed," she informed him.

"Yeah?" With some alarm, he noted her toes tap-dancing up the bookshelves, threatening to dislodge any number of paperbacks.

"I mean it. I seriously reformed. I woke up one morning and realized I was causing my parents' ulcers. I haven't been a hellion in *years,* Sam. I went to college, brought my parents back all A's. No parties, no nonsense, no more disappointing them. Ron was a blue-blood Boston Brahman, spotless background, never spilled catsup on his tie, had his own money...hell, he nearly came with a halo. My parents *dreamed* of my bringing home someone like Ron, and I was on a roll about this being good business. When we settled in, I worked with the Red Cross, volunteered at the library and the local church. Only everyone's forgotten that now. When things started going wrong, the only thing anybody wanted to remember was my past history as a hellion—what are you doing?"

"Trying to put your shoes on." No small job, when her toes were still weaving midair. "I think, Red, that I should have taken you home about twenty minutes ago. Not that I want you to stop talking, but let's just see how you are right now, okay?''

Once he fitted her shoes on, he slowly, very slowly, pulled her to her feet. It was the first time he'd touched her. Her fragile bones . . . he remembered them. He remembered how tiny she was next to him, remembered the texture of her springy russet hair in his hands, remembered her scent, remembered the rose blush of her lips. But he didn't remember—because it had never happened before—Val ever looking at him with such innocent, beguiling, total trust.

His darling was regrettably and dizzily bombed out of her mind.

''I feel a little strange,'' Val confessed. And then pitched forward straight into his chest.

Sam figured she was going to kill him tomorrow— assuming she'd even speak to him—but he didn't immediately have time to worry about it. Their dinner debris had been stashed in a waste-basket, but he couldn't carry her and dispose of the wine bottle and glasses at the same time. Somewhere, she had a purse. And probably a sweater or jacket. And then there was the problem of wheels. He had to drive her car; otherwise she wouldn't have transportation in the morning, and he could easily hike the couple of miles back from her house to pick up the Mustang. But what was she driving, and where on earth was it parked?

The last problem took care of itself, since there was only one car in the back alley that late and her keys fit it. By the time he folded her into the passenger seat of the little blue Escort, Valentine was snoring—little catchy, breathy snores. Thankfully the alley was deserted, he thought, as Val might not have appreciated being carried in front of any onlookers. Her neighbors were likely to get the wrong idea. From everything she'd told him, they already had too many wrong ideas about Val.

He checked on her as he started the engine. She was curled up like a baby, but her blouse gaped open, revealing a milk-white throat and the lace trim of a pink camisole. Her hair was a tangled cape; one high heel had slipped off again; pale lashes brushed her cheeks and her lips were parted in a sensual smile. She looked as if she'd just spent forty-eight hours with a demanding lover.

Sam wished she had. And that the lover had been him.

On the short drive to her house, he mentally evaluated everything she'd told him. The town's attitude toward her, he understood now, had been the dragon on her tail in the Gulf. What he couldn't understand is why Val had come home. She was ashamed of marrying the jerk. He got that. But the solution of dealing with a small-minded small-town seemed so easy: Move. Relocate. Start fresh. Someplace, anyplace, where people would appreciate her fun-loving, impulsive, hellion streak—instead of putting her down for it.

By nature Sam was a pacifist, not a fighter, but he'd been raised with a concept of honor. When someone was in trouble, you helped. When you had the ways and the means to stop someone vulnerable from getting hurt, you simply did it, no fanfare, no discussion.

It was tempting, damn tempting, to envision blindfolding, gagging and handcuffing Valentine and simply riding her out of town. Chicago was no ivory tower, but his redhead didn't need an ivory tower. She was plenty tough, plenty sassy, plenty stubborn. She'd thrive just fine, maybe even rediscover that lost hellion streak. And nobody'd hurt her in Chicago, because he'd level them first.

That plan was incredibly appealing, until he imagined the unfortunate moment when he would have to remove the blindfold, the gag, the handcuffs.

Val, doubtless, would come at him spitting nails. His redhead wasn't exactly looking for a hero. In fact, she had enough pride to match ten women—or men. Conceivably a lover could get through to her.

But he wasn't her lover.

Yet.

At her house, he didn't douse the car lights until he'd filched through her purse for the house key. En route, he discovered the wallet in her purse and squinted at it. Six dollars, thirty-seven cents. No credit cards. A driver's licence picture that made her look like a thirteen-year-old nun. Also in her purse was a checkbook that, when he held it up to the light, revealed a balance of eighty-three dollars.

His jaw muscles tightened. He shut off the car lights, slammed the door on his side and strode around to open hers. Val melted out like poured butter, straight into his arms. He scooped her up, kneed the car door shut and headed straight for her front door.

The entrance was still guarded, he promptly discovered, by her belligerent bat-carrying protector sitting on the porch steps in the dark. "What'd you do to my Val?"

"Nothing. She's asleep, and I'm taking her in the house to put her to bed. Go home, Lincoln." He brushed past the sleepy-eyed urchin, then hesitated. "You have a home?"

"Sure I have a home. But I don't leave here until Miz Shroeder's okay. Ever."

"Your father's probably worried about you."

"My father ain't worried about me. He could care. He cut out on me and my mom and the rest of us a hundred years ago."

Sam hesitated again. "Then your mom's probably worried about you."

"My mom works nights, and if I stayed at Miz Shroeder's it wouldn't be the first time so she wouldn't worry about it either way. You, now. You need to worry. Because if you done something to my Val—"

"Lincoln, if you'll take a look, you'll see there's nothing wrong with her. She's sleeping, and all I'm trying to do is put her to bed. Would you try and trust me?"

"Why should I?"

In spite of impossible odds, Sam thought, he was starting to like the boy. "Because I care about her even more than you do," he answered him shortly, and moved on.

He managed to get the key into the front door lock without any help from Lincoln, but inside was tougher going. There wasn't a light on in the entire house, and although Val was a lightweight hundred pounds, carrying her in the dark through an unfamiliar house was tricky.

The layout of the place gradually became clear. The tiled-floor entrance led to a kitchen on his left, and the length of a Florida room/living room on his right. He aimed right, figuring that was the surest route to the back rooms. His shin connected with the sharp edge of a coffee table, and then the body obstacle of a fig plant bigger than a tree. Her hair tangled in the fig plant's leaves. When he stopped to untangle her, his dogged sidekick stepped on his heels.

"You could help a lot," he said dryly to Lincoln, "by turning on a lamp."

"I don't think I should have let you in the house," Lincoln said, "and I *sure* don't think you should be going any further."

Sam's fondness for the kid was growing by leaps and bounds. Whether Val wanted to or not, he sincerely doubted that she'd been able to entertain many men friends, hampered by such a tactful and dedicated chaperon. "Lincoln," he said reasonably, "I have to take her to the bedroom. How else can I put her to bed?"

Beyond the long living room was the dim glow of a night-light, coming from the bathroom. It smelled like her store, vanilla mixed with scent and the drift of roses. In the same hall off the bathroom were two rooms. The one might have been intended for a bedroom, but Sam caught the bulky shadow of a file cabinet and the gleam of a polished desk—she was obviously using it as an office.

In the last room, glass doors led to an outside patio; they also let in the bright shine of moonlight. Even without artificial light, he could see the quilted expanse of a double bed, a tall white wardrobe of Victorian style, and a round wicker chair stuffed with cushions. There was no tiled floor here, but the thick muffle of a shaggy white carpet. A dozen candlesticks nestled in a small mirrored table, each a different size and shape and holding a variety of scented candles. The mirrored surface of the table captured the moonlight's reflection. He could easily imagine the candles all lit, Val in bed, making love with her by that blaze of soft light.

The fantasy was necessarily brief.

"Like what's the holdup here," Lincoln said impatiently. "You put her down, then go away. I'll cover her up. You don't need to stick around."

"No," Sam said absently.

"What'd you mean, *no?* You think I won't use this bat—?"

"I'm going to put her to bed. Me, not you. And what you're going to do—if you want to help her—is go out to her car and get her purse and sweater. And her shoe. Somewhere on the floor of the car, there's one navy blue high-heeled shoe. She could need all that stuff tomorrow, so you think you could handle that?"

Lincoln was eventually persuaded to see the advantages of cooperation.

Alone with her, knowing he didn't have long, Sam laid her on the quilted comforter. After taking off her one shoe, he unbuttoned and unzipped her skirt. She could sleep in the blouse and rest of her underwear, but the slim-styled skirt would have constricted any natural movement.

When he tugged the skirt down her hips, though, his whole body tightened with desire. There was no excuse. It wasn't as if she were naked. She still had a million clothes on, it was dark, he never even touched her bare skin. Still, that flush of heat, of pure raw wanting, was powerful enough to make him catch his breath.

Sam had desired other women before, had pursued and won his share. Some men shied at commitment;

he never had. He'd never started a relationship where
the chemistry wasn't mutual and right, where the relationship didn't have a good chance of a future. Sam
wanted a mate, not just a lover. He'd *wanted* to be
hooked. It just never seemed to happen.

He'd been hooked on Val from the day he met her.
Hook, line and sinkered. Nervous with her when he
hadn't been nervous around a woman in years. Desperate to be with her, in a constant state of heat, anxious and edgy when they were apart—the overall
symptoms had been so humorous that, in the Gulf,
he'd thought he was losing his mind. And didn't care.

Sam had searched too long for a woman who made
him feel that way. He wasn't about to let it go, and as
he folded Val between the cool sheets, he was fiercely
tempted to slide in beside her. Not to make love—
she'd had too much wine, and he'd never take advantage of Val that way. But it was hard to deny himself
the right to hold her, touch her, sleep with her wrapped
in his arms. He'd come months; he'd come miles. God
knows where he was even going to find a place to stay
tonight, and the only place he wanted to stay—or be—
was with her.

But Valentine would probably greet him with a
shotgun if she woke and found him next to her. Assuming Lincoln didn't bash him with the baseball bat
first.

He tucked the blanket around her chin, smoothed
back her hair and then leaned closer. For an instant,
he did nothing, just studied her pale, moonlit face.
And then he bent down and kissed her, softly, just
once, with more promise than pressure, more hint
than substance of the emotions he felt. Her lips yielded

for the imprint of his, responsive even in sleep, and she murmured something sweet and whispery.

Before she could waken, though, he straightened back up.

He'd found her.

For tonight, that would have to be enough.

Three

―――

The Florida morning sun was painfully bright. Gingerly, very gingerly, Val unlocked the back door of the store. Inside was blessed dimness. Her head felt as if it were squeezed in a vise, and even after drinking two glasses of orange juice, her throat was still as parched as Death Valley.

It wasn't her first hangover. Val had a clear recollection of experimenting with the contents of her father's liquor cabinet when she was fifteen. That singular experience had cured her of any desire to overindulge. Being a convivial host, Randolph Shroeder stocked everything from fancy liqueurs and wines to the usual bourbon, whiskey, Scotch and gin. Motivated by curiosity, she'd sampled a little of everything—and been sick as a dog.

Val dropped her purse in the back office and promptly filled the coffee machine. The major difference between the two experiences was that at fifteen, she'd had the brains and judgment of a witless goose. At twenty-eight, she no longer had that helpful excuse.

It was enormously tempting to blame Sam. He had, after all, deliberately and manipulatively sneaked all that wine on her. But Val knew where the real fault belonged. Several times she remembered being surprised that her glass was still full, but she hadn't paid attention. She'd been too busy talking, too busy inventing wholesale lies about how wonderfully the bookstore was doing.

If that was all she remembered, Val wouldn't mind. Unfortunately, she had disgustingly lucid memories of spilling her problems on Sam. Worse yet, she had another nasty, crystal-clear memory of the texture of Sam's mouth moving over hers, his hand on her cheek, his eyes open and shining in the moonlit shadows. The moonlit shadows of—Lord!—her own bedroom.

Glumly Val fumbled in her lower desk drawer for a bottle of aspirin. She found it and popped two, dry, thinking that other women never seemed to get themselves into messes as she did. Other women seemed to lead good, responsible, respectable lives without even trying. She tried. It just never seemed to do any good.

God, she hoped Sam had flown back to Chicago last night.

The coffee machine finished brewing. As she reached for a mug, she heard a hearty pounding on the door in front. The sound was loud enough to renew her rattling headache, but she jerked to her feet. The front entrance was still locked. There was a remote chance that she had a customer.

She should have known better. As quickly as she pulled up the shade and unlocked the door, the town sheriff lumbered inside.

"You okay? I started to worry when I didn't see the store lights come on. It's ten past nine."

"I'm fine. I just got a late start this morning." Val closed the door behind him. Harold Wilson was sixty-two and shaped like a tank, with a full head of grizzly gray hair and a road map of worry lines on his face. He'd earned every wrinkle. Chekapee didn't have much of a criminal element, but he'd raised seven kids.

Val had known of him from the day she was born. She hadn't personally met him, though, until the night he caught her stealing the license plates off his car on a dare. She must have been around fourteen, and positive he was going to send her to San Quentin. His stern, lengthy lecture had been interrupted by several coughing fits that she only later realized were an effort to suppress his laughter.

Harold, unlike everyone else in town, never seemed to think she was guilty of anything but irrepressible high spirits and terrible judgment. During Ron's trial, when no one else was speaking to her, he'd stop by the house and demand coffee. At a time when she couldn't possibly need more problems, Harold had landed her with Lincoln. And then Jonesey.

"You sure you're okay?" Harold peered at her face. "You don't look so hot. Pale. You're not catching Jonesey's flu, are you?"

"No flu. Just a teensy headache."

"You gotta quit running at a hundred miles an hour. I keep telling you. When's Jonesey due back at work?"

Harold knew where her coffee machine was—he claimed it was the prerogative of the sheriff to filch free coffee—and he ambled back from her office with a full mug. Val suspicioned there was more on his mind than his ritual coffee break, but for a time she kept him busy chitchatting about the progress of Jonesey's physical and mental health.

Bartholomew Jones was fifty-five, and had been a hardworking, community-active churchgoer until his wife died. Then he started shoplifting, for reasons no one could fathom. He never stole anything he needed and always had the money to pay for it. The sheriff hadn't known what to do with him. In a big city, by the third offense, Jonesey would probably have been thrown in jail. Harold sent him to work for Val in the store—thirty days of penance that was long over—but Jonesey had stuck. Guilt chewed on Val's conscience for taking advantage. She couldn't afford to pay him. Jonesey claimed he had enough to eat, he now got free books to read, and she couldn't keep the damn store open sixty hours a week without help. The sheriff agreed that she was being a dolt. Jonesey was no longer shoplifting. Harold was thrilled with the whole situation.

Val was thrilled that the conversation lingered nicely on Jonesey, but she should have known that her good luck couldn't last. Harold checked on her most mornings, but most mornings he eventually remembered that the safety and welfare of Chekapee was the reason he had a taxpayer-paid badge. Not today. Hunched over her counter with his second mug of coffee, the sheriff genially smiled at her.

"So," he drawled out, "I heard you had a visitor yesterday."

Val thought darkly that gossip traveled faster in Chekapee than measles in a grade school. "I think a speeder just went by," she said. "Must have been going fifty, and right down River Street. Looked like a big juicy potential ticket to me."

Harold didn't even have the courtesy to glance out the window. "I heard it was a man."

"An acquaintance," Val immediately qualified. "Just someone I met in the Gulf."

"The ladies been saying that he's quite a looker. Got a couple of years on you, but not too old. Left a pretty fancy plane in the hangar. Owns his own business, I heard, Shepherd Air Freight out of Chicago. Real fussy about his plane, Hosh told me. You know Hosh, the mechanic at the—"

"Forget it, Sheriff."

"Forget what?"

"Forget what you're thinking." The aspirin wasn't working. The invisible bear rattling his cage in her head was only getting worse. "He's just a friend. He just stopped by for a short visit. In fact, I expect he's already flown back home—"

"He checked in last night at the Lazy Day Motel," Harold informed her amiably, and watched her face flush with sudden hectic color. He scratched the whiskers on his chin. "Big brown eyes, that's what Mabel said. Shoulders like a linebacker. Made me kinda wonder if he knew you were divorced from Rat Bait."

"It wouldn't make any difference if I were a four-time bigamist. He's just a casual friend," Val said firmly.

"Hmm." Harold finally set down his coffee mug, reached for his hat and rambled toward the door.

"Don't know many men who'd fly into town just to casually visit with a friend. It'd seem to indicate a fairly serious interest to me. Course, maybe he had other business in Chekapee. For all I know, he could be dying to raise oranges...why, honey, the way you're holding open that door, I'm inclined to think you're anxious to get rid of me."

"Nonsense. You know I love you." Val pecked him on the cheek—his feelings would have been hurt if she hadn't—and then thankfully watched him meander down River Street. Even when the sheriff was gone, though, the subject of their conversation lingered in her mind like a nagging toothache.

Sam had never been supposed to find her. But he had. And unless she stuck her head in the sand like an ostrich, Val could hardly pretend that he'd flown all the way to Chekapee because he was dying to raise oranges.

He'd come for her. Even after all these months, even after all the lectures and warnings she'd given him, even after telling him straight out to find someone else. Tarnation. What did a woman have to do to convince the damn man that she wasn't interested?

Not kiss him back, suggested the nasty little voice of her conscience.

And it was true she had a shamelessly guilty history of kissing him back. Last night, even zonked to her back teeth, she'd responded to Sam's closeness. And in the Gulf, she'd discovered that Shepherd had a crippling effect on her inhibitions, her good sense, her moral values...hell. She'd wanted the blasted man beyond rhyme or reason.

Still did.

But that was neither here nor there. Alone in the store, Val rearranged the display in her front window and then took a dust cloth to the bookshelves, although her mind was on none of the usual chores.

Her ex-husband had already been in jail when the Gulf War broke out. When she'd volunteered with the Red Cross, no one in Chekapee had expected her to come back. The house where she'd lived with Ron was sold. Her parents' country home was kept open, but since the banking debacle, they'd spent most of their time at the condo in Ormond Beach. There wasn't a Shroeder left in town except for her—no reason for her to come back—and, heaven knows, she hadn't wanted to.

It would have been easy to relocate, easy to start over anyplace where people didn't know her. Unfortunately, that option would have meant living with a cloud over her head for the rest of her life. If she deserted ship, the townspeople would always believe she was guilty, or partly guilty, for what her ex-husband had done.

Val *had* to stay, if she was ever going to prove that she had nothing to be ashamed of, and she'd anticipated that the bookstore would have a rocky start. It took time and action to change people's minds. For months now, she'd kept the store open sixty hours a week, and still managed to volunteer at the church and the local Red Cross. She dressed prim as a nun, smiled at anyone who snubbed her, lived chaste as a saint.

Unfortunately, the store was going down and she was going broke and none of it was working. Val thought glumly that she should have expected no less. There seemed to be something intrinsically wrong with her. A wicked streak. An offbeat gene. From her teenage pranks to her choice of a husband, she'd always made huge mistakes, never little ones. It was a tad tricky to convince people she had nothing to be ashamed of when she didn't believe it herself. Val had been a disappointment to everyone in her life as far back as she could remember.

The only exception was Sam.

From the day she'd met him, Shepherd had treated her like something special. A good woman. The kind of woman that a man instinctively respected and protected. That idiotic attitude of his, though he couldn't know it, had given her the strength and courage to come home. Alone. The only way it could be. She never wanted Sam anywhere near her problems. She had too long a history of screwing up everything that mattered to her. She could face her own music.

But she couldn't, simply couldn't, face the risk of being a disappointment to Sam.

If Shepherd was still in town, she simply had to convince him to go home.

Sam wandered into the bookstore midafternoon. He spotted Val behind the counter. Her head shot up the instant the bells tinkled, but her attention was momentarily distracted by a customer. That was okay by him. He suspected he was in deep dutch because of the wine, and a cash-paying customer might put her in a good mood.

The carpet muffled his footsteps as he sauntered behind a bookshelf, where he had a clear view of her over a lid of ethnic cookbooks. Valentine seemed to be dressed for a church bazaar, in a high-necked blouse with a cameo at the throat and her hair all scraped back in a coil of hairpins. But Sam couldn't care less what she was wearing.

Like a miser for gold, his gaze latched onto her face and hoarded every detail. The white lines of exhaustion had disappeared. The bruised shadows under her eyes—gone, too. Her skin was still translucent, but natural color streaked her cheeks and her hazel eyes sparkled with life and animation. Instead of suffering any aftereffects from an evening of tippling, she looked as if she'd had a wonderfully restful night's sleep.

Which amply justified, Sam thought righteously, his helping hand with that little bit of wine the night before.

His view of her, unfortunately, kept getting blocked. Not by the hills and valleys of cookbooks at his nose height, but by her customer. The older woman was a rawboned six feet, dressed in beige polyester, with straggly gray hair yanked behind small pointy ears and spectacles perched on a nonexistent nose. It was the ears that made Sam think of a bat, but that was before he caught wind of the conversation. The older woman wasn't only a bat, but of the vampire species.

"I would hardly be here if I didn't have a choice." The old bat pushed up her lenses. "I want to make that perfectly clear."

His Valentine didn't seem to notice the insult. "Just glad I could be of help, Miss Holmes."

"I ordered the copies of *Lear* from the publisher. If they'd come in on time, I would never have come here. But I can hardly start the Shakespearean unit on Monday without copies of the play."

"Eighteen copies, wasn't it?" Val punched the numbers on the cash register.

Miss Holmes scowled down at her. "I still don't understand how you happened to have so many in stock—"

"One of the kids in your class happened to mention that you were having trouble. I ordered extras just in case."

Sam waited to hear a thank-you, but apparently the old bat had never heard of manners. "I might as well be honest with you, Valerie. This was a singular experience. It hardly means that I intend to patronize your store."

"No problem, Miss Holmes. I appreciate your stopping in."

A check changed hands. The dowager picked up her bag of books. Sniffed. Opened the door to the cheerful jingle of bells, and stalked out.

Silence followed. When Val walked into the cookbook aisle, Sam happened to be in the history section. When she walked past the history shelves, he happened to be in agriculture. When she caught up with him, he happened to be leaning against the counter by the cash register, with books stacked halfway to the ceiling.

He meant to say "hi," really lazily, really casually, and then explain that he'd coaxed the wine into her because she looked so tired and as if she needed a good night's sleep.

Instead he said, "If I were you, I'd have decked that old bag. How come you put up with that horse manure?"

Val met his eyes squarely. "Miss Holmes is the English teacher at the high school. Her salary is her whole income. Her parents left her a big trust, security, a future, that turned into nothing because of my ex-husband.'' As if that explained everything and the discussion was closed, she motioned to the mountain of her books on her counter. ''What's this?''

''I like to read,'' Sam confessed in his most disarming tenor.

''Yeah?'' Val efficiently sorted through the books, making two piles. In one pile, there was the French, Italian and Hungarian cookbooks, the twelve-book series on the Civil War, the treatise on the fruit moth affecting orange grove production, and the hardbound self-help book *Living With Arthritis*. Left over was a single cheap paperback spy thriller. She hefted the paperback, shook her head. ''There's better stuff out than this, Sam.''

He followed her back to the thriller section. In a matter of seconds, she'd searched the shelves and come up with three action spy adventures. She knew her business; she'd picked out the best—not that Sam was about to admit that he'd already read them. ''I want the other books, too.''

''Sure, you do,'' she said dryly.

''Honest. I have a brother, Cole. He's really into Civil War history. And my sister-in-law likes to cook. And I have a friend who has a terrible case of arthritis—''

''Fine. If you want those books, they're on the house.'' She sashayed neatly behind the counter and poised her fingers on the cash register keys. ''Did you want me to ring up the paperbacks?''

Sam dug into his back pocket for his wallet before the darn fool woman could try to offer him those free, too. He handed her a twenty. She meticulously counted out his change and bagged his books. ''I don't suppose there's a chance you're hungry?" he asked casually.

"Not right now, but thanks."

"Later then. What time do you usually break for dinner?"

"Usually I break around five—I have a man, Bartholomew Jones, who takes most of the afternoon hours and Saturdays. But Jonesey's out with the flu, which means that the best I can do is grab a sandwich here."

"So what time do you want me to bring sandwiches in?"

"Sam." She took a huge breath. "Maybe we'd better talk about why you came here."

Sam was fairly sure he'd rather talk about sandwiches.

She picked her words with painstaking care. "I haven't been out with anyone. It isn't just you. You have to know that I care about you... but it's just the wrong time for me to be involved with anyone. I have some problems in my life right now. They're important to me. And until I've handled them, I honestly can't be involved."

"I can understand that," Sam said soothingly. Poor baby, there was a terrible catch in her throat. She was trying so hard to be honest, to let him down gently.

"I don't want to hurt you, Sam."

"It's okay, honey."

"A relationship—a good relationship—takes time and energy."

"I agree."

"I just don't have that time and energy right now. There are things I have to resolve, on my own, alone.

You can't do it for me. You can't do it with me. So honestly, it would just be better if you—''

He strode around the counter in three long strides. ''I can see you're getting all upset . . . and for no reason, Valentine. I never came here to upset you. This is all real easy. If you want me to leave, I'll leave.''

Immediately the anxious look disappeared from her eyes. Her shoulders were still tense, but when his big hands slowly skated up her arms, some of that tension disappeared, too. He smiled for her. When she tentatively smiled back, lashes studded her cheeks softer than velvet.

''But do you think, maybe, that you could spare a kiss for an old friend before he goes?'' he murmured.

He could have waited for her permission, but when she didn't instantly pull away, he took that as permission enough. Her face was already lifted toward him. All he had to do was duck down and angle his head.

Her lips were as butter soft as he remembered, the taste of her just as intoxicating. The kiss last night had been unsatisfying to the point of aggravation—he wasn't sure if Val even knew it was him.

She knew it was him now.

Her fingers closed on his wrists like repressive little manacles, as if she could control the kiss by controlling his hands. But he didn't try to touch her. At least with his hands.

He moved his mouth over hers slowly. As though he needed this kiss to last him. As if he was actually saying goodbye. When his tongue touched the tip of hers, she made a sound, a winsome, lonely sound, and suddenly she was kissing him back. Wildly. Desperately. She forgot about holding his wrists. Her hands climbed his arms and tightly lassoed his neck.

He leaned back against the counter, drawing her with him, pulling her into the wedge of his thighs. Some strange metal edge jabbed into his spine. He didn't care. Anybody could walk in. He didn't care about that, either.

One kiss melted into another, then another. Never mind what she said, his redhead had missed him. Her lips were smooth and soft and mobile under his, and he remembered her precious responsiveness. Desire, sizzle sharp, raced through his blood at the feel of her breasts snuggled against his chest. She smelled like vanilla and rain-wet roses. She kissed like the most vulnerable woman ever born, as no other woman had ever kissed him. She was his.

She had to be his.

He ran his hands down her shoulders, gently, tenderly, before breaking off the kiss and lifting his head to look at her. A spare breath dragged from her lungs. Her lips were wet and red, her eyes a stunned cloudy topaz. She lifted a hand, and he saw her fingers were trembling.

"I shouldn't have...I never meant to..." Her whisper was achingly soft. "Sam, you *have* to go."

He dropped his hands. "I'm leaving, honey. Right now."

Four

Sam had no intention of going anywhere.

His father had taught him to never argue with a woman. It was a philosophy Sam strongly adhered to, especially in Val's case. She was just going to get all touchy and nervous and upset if they argued about his staying. She'd probably lie to him again, and Sam couldn't see putting her through all that. It wasn't as if she could win. Nothing short of a bomb—not after that kiss—was likely to change his mind.

In a matter of hours, she was obviously going to discover that he was still around. But later was definitely better. Sam had no desire to face that redheaded temper until he had to, and before that, he needed answers. So far he didn't have any more than a wine-befuddled account of the trouble she was in.

He pulled into her driveway around four o'clock. As he'd expected, a small face peered through the front window to check him out, even before Sam turned off the engine. Slowly he pocketed the car keys and ambled up the sidewalk. By the time he reached the porch, Lincoln had most handily flung open the front door.

"For cripes' *sake,*" the urchin said disgustedly. "I thought we got rid of you yesterday."

"Afraid I'm pretty hard to get rid of." Sam moved in and straight past the boy, calling over his shoulder, "Come on, Linc. You and I have work to do. I need your help."

"What work? What help? And geezle beezle, how many times do I got to tell you—you *can't* go in the house."

One of Sam's immediate goals was making friends with the three-foot delinquent, but momentarily he was distracted. Last night, the house had been too pitch-dark for him to notice much. In broad daylight, the place revealed more about Val than anything she'd told him.

His destination was the kitchen, but he caught a quick glimpse of the long living room. It was bright, warm, welcoming, and immediately worried him. A couch, chair and coffee table sum-totaled her furniture. The wild profusion of plants didn't begin to fill the empty spaces. She'd made the coffee table from a piece of driftwood—his shins intimately remembered connecting with that driftwood the night before—and she'd reupholstered the couch and chair in a perky yellow print that failed to disguise sagging springs. The tile floor shone and the windows gleamed, but all Sam could think was dammit, she didn't have a dime. The only thing his redhead had spent money on was paint, because she'd followed through with that perky sunny yellow on every wall surface from the hall to the kitchen.

The kitchen was all aclutter: white Formica, white tile, copper pots hanging over a fifties-style stove, a bitsy glass-topped table. Schoolbooks, presumedly Lincoln's, were spread out on the table, but the giant life-size dummy draped in a chair had to belong to Val. The dummy's name was "Darling," according to the printing on his chest, and Sam guessed that Val taught first aid, because the dummy was the standard Red Cross model used to practice artificial resuscitation. There was barely room to turn around even without Darling, and her counters were piled high with a range of debris from rolled bandages to sheet music—all church hymns.

Sam opened the refrigerator, then her freezer, then hunkered down by her cupboards. The longer he looked, the more his jaw tightened.

When he'd carried her in last night, his mind had been on how good she felt, how right, how fiercely he wanted her. During their embrace in the bookstore, he hadn't given a holy damn about anything except the texture of her sweet-soft mouth and the heady awareness that she was coming alive for him, apart for him.

He should have been paying more attention to her bones. Val was squirt size to start, but not fragile. At least not this fragile. She'd lost weight, and the balance in her checkbook wasn't enough to buy a rug for her floor, much less keep her in peanut butter.

"Whatch ya think you're doin', man? You stay out of her stuff or I'm warning you, you're gonna be dead meat."

Sam lifted his head. He'd never meant to ignore the boy this long. In spite of the violent warning, the kid hadn't budged from the doorway and his eyes were all worried and anxious. "Do you know how to write?" Sam asked him.

Those thin shoulders immediately bristled. "What you think, I'm some kind of dummy? I'm in fourth grade. Course, I can write."

"Good." Sam dove into his shirt pocket and came up with a pencil and small pad of paper. "I need you to help me make a list, and then we're going to get something to eat in this damn house besides soup."

For a moment the child forgot to be belligerent. His eyes widened. "We?" he echoed. "You mean . . . you and me? Going out someplace, like in that car?"

"You and me," Sam affirmed. "In the Mustang." Watching the boy's eyes, he added, "With the top down. There's no way I could possibly find a grocery store without your help, and Linc, I'm telling you straight we need to get some meat on her bones."

"Meat on her bones," Lincoln echoed.

"She needs ice cream. She needs cookies. You could help me find that stuff, couldn't you? Assuming you can go with me. I don't know who you need to get permission from—"

"Permission is no sweat," Lincoln assured him. "I don't need permission from nobody to do nothing. You can ask Mrs. Meacham. You can ask anybody. I'm incorrigible."

Lincoln had apparently heard the word often and considered the epitaph a major source of pride. Initially Sam had been afraid the child wouldn't talk to him. By the time they'd cruised town in the open convertible and were winging a cart through the grocery store, the urchin had yet to shut up. Sam picked up enough bits and pieces to understand that Linc had begun a career in trouble when his father deserted the family. The mother was working two jobs to make ends meet and had no way to supervise the boy. The local sheriff had intervened when Linc was caught stealing money from a teacher's purse at the desperado age of eight going on nine. He was a tad young to send to reform school, and apparently the sheriff had suckered Val into taking on the "incorrigible devil." His job, after school, was looking after her and protecting her house.

"She's got a lot of people mad at her," Linc told him matter-of-factly when they were unloading groceries back at the house. "I know what that's like. People used to be mad at me all the time. So we stick together, Val and me."

Sam stacked T-bones in her freezer and fresh food on her refrigerator shelves, the whole time listening, listening, listening. The kid was more dangerous than a sliver. He'd liked the urchin on sight and had hoped to make friends with him, but he hadn't expected the newfound trust shining in Lincoln's eyes to get under his skin. Sam hadn't done anything to earn that trust, not with Linc. Nor with Val.

Yet.

"Man, is she gonna be surprised with all this food," Lincoln said fervently.

"Hmm." Sam folded the last grocery bag, sincerely doubting that Valentine's reaction to the food would be as mild as *surprise*. She was going to be ticked that he was still in town, and bloody ticked that he'd been nosily interfering in her life. "Val isn't going to be home until after the store closes. How late are you supposed to stick around?" he asked Lincoln.

"Six. No later. Val called and told me I stayed too late last night. And I *knew* I was staying too late, but I didn't know what time she was coming home with Jonesey out sick, and it's my job to make sure she gets safe in the house. I mean, we're talking *confusing*. How was I s'posed to know the right thing to do?"

"You had a tricky problem," Sam said gravely, "but you don't have to worry about it tonight. I have to go out for a while. But you go home when she told you, and I'll be back to be sure she gets safely in the house."

"That'd be a load off my mind," Lincoln confessed.

Sam wished the load on his mind was so easily fixed. Plucking the car keys from his pocket, he headed out. He took a left on River and aimed vaguely out of town, unsure where the open road led and not caring. Before seeing Val again, he needed some time alone, and he'd always done his best thinking behind a wheel.

The convertible top was down; wind whipped through his hair and stung his cheeks, but the drive didn't seem to help. Frustration still gnawed on his nerves. Stocking Val's kitchen with a few groceries was like plugging a hole in a dike with a sponge. He knew how to feed her, but damned if he knew how to *help* her.

The problem, Sam thought gloomily, was that he couldn't even identify the damn problem. He understood that she'd been married to a jerk, that she was caught up in a small-town scandal, and that she wasn't going to allow *love* in her vocabulary until she'd resolved something. Only *what* was this mysterious something that was so terribly important to her? Her bookstore appeared to be going down at the speed of sound, and his damned pint-sized redhead appeared to be starving for a principle that Sam couldn't identify for love or money.

Absently he noticed the police car trailing him. Then forgot it. His mind scrolled back to the way she'd kissed him—as if he was the only life raft in a lonely ocean, as though he was the only man in her universe. He'd loved that kiss. He'd taken heart from that kiss. But damned if it was helping him figure out what to *do* for her.

A flashing red light reflected in his rearview mirror. Again Sam glanced at the police car, but he already knew he was driving five miles under the limit. He assumed the cop was after other prey... until he heard the whine of a siren and discovered the police car riding directly on his tail.

The black-topped highway was nearly deserted where Sam braked off the shoulder. Orange groves dotted the landscape, their dark green leaves shining in the late afternoon sun. Impatiently Sam snapped off the key. His family had been peppered with men in law enforcement; he'd lived around cops his whole childhood. He had no problem about talking to the cop, beyond annoyance at the waste of time.

Through his rearview mirror, Sam watched the man climb out of the car. His curiosity was aroused when he caught the glint of a sheriff's badge. Suddenly he didn't mind the encounter. If this was the sheriff who knew both Val and Lincoln, Sam was predisposed to like him.

That predisposition lasted all of thirty seconds.

The sheriff adjusted his hat, hitched up his trousers and ambled over to Sam's window. "I clocked you at twenty miles over. Let's see your license and registration."

Sam shot him a disbelieving look. The older man was built like a tank, with a leathered, weathered face, intelligent eyes, and a full head of grizzly gray hair under the sheriff's hat. The guy didn't *look* daft. "This is a rental car," Sam told him, "so I can't swear the speedometer is accurate, because I don't know. But I know cars. And I know how to drive. And there isn't a chance in a blue moon that I was doing twenty miles over."

"So you say. Let's see the license and registration."

Sam pulled out his wallet and fumbled in the glove box, hoping like hell that the registration was in there. It was. The sheriff took the documents and propped his burly arms on the window ledge.

"So, you're a Northerner? And from Chicago yet. Big city, Chicago. Are you married, Mr. Shepherd?"

Sam studied him again, this time more carefully. Something was going on here. The older man hadn't glanced at either the registration or the license. "No."

"Ever been married?"

"No." Sam added dryly, "Is there some miraculous relevance between my marital status and the price of a speeding ticket?"

The sheriff didn't appear to notice his ironic attempt at humor. He hitched up his trousers again. "We've had some trouble in this town. Made it difficult for some of us to trust a stranger appearing out of the blue. Possibly if I explained about that trouble, you'd understand why some of us tend toward being cautious."

Sam stared at those old shrewd eyes and then slowly opened the door. He stepped out of the car, his gaze still focused on the sheriff's face. "I heard something about that trouble," he said carefully. "Something about an embezzler, wasn't it?"

"Right. The Shroeder family ran our bank around here for several generations. You happen to know any Shroeders?"

"Val."

"No kidding?" The sheriff stroked his chin as if amazed, and then cheerfully rambled on. "Well, it was a small family-owned bank, see. So small they never bothered being covered by FDIC insurance, which never worried none of us. The bank stayed open during the Depression, through all the iddly-piddly recessions since, so nobody worried that it was going down. You following me so far, Mr. Shepherd?"

"I'm following you."

"I thought you might be. Anyhow, the point is that our bank was real small, real solid, real secure... but conceivably old-fashioned in its management. And Val happened to marry a nice young man from the North. A good-looker, that Ron, nice boy, nice manners, and a fancy MBA in economics. Val's father figured it was time the bank entered the twentieth century, tried him out, saw how bright he was, and made him an investment officer. You still following me, Mr. Shepherd?"

"I'm still following you." A pickup truck zoomed by with a rattling noisy muffler. Sam didn't glance at it and neither, he noticed, did his unexpected friend.

"It was two years before anyone noticed anything wrong. That Ron had computer printouts up the wazoo showing how good all those 'investments' were doing. And he came from money. He *had* money, so there was no reason to guess he'd steal when he was already rolling in it. In fact, nobody would have likely known for a long time after that if it wasn't for Val.''

"Val?"

The sheriff glanced away, as if he were appreciating the gold ball of a sun perched above the nest of citrus groves. "The day she brought me a briefcase full of stuff, her face was white as a sheet and she was shaking like she had a fever. I'm not likely to forget that day. I guess she'd suspected for a while—apparently her husband was getting some pretty strange phone calls at home—but when she tried to confront him, he always had a good story. Eventually she put it together and confronted him again. He told her then. He also told her that he needed some time to fix it, that he never intended to keep the money but just to play with it, that nobody'd ever know if she just kept quiet. Val, thank God, had the sense not to trust the rat by then.'' The sheriff paused. "Of course, if you've been around Chekapee long, you've probably heard that some think Val was in cahoots with her ex.''

"I've heard," Sam agreed.

"Folks have a tendency to be blind where money's concerned. You ever notice that?''

"I've noticed that.''

The sheriff pulled off his hat, ran a hand through his hair. "Most folks around here have also tended to forget that we all trusted—and *liked*—that rat bait she married. Me included, and I consider myself a fair judge of character. He just never did anything to make anyone suspect he was a snake in the grass. Of course, a marriage is different. That's what people keep thinking—that living with a man, day in, day out, she had to see the other side of him. She had to *know*.''

The sheriff plopped on his hat again. "Myself now, I'm inclined to believe that when a girl's been led to think of herself as a disappointment her whole life . . . well. I just think it's possible that she was always so busy looking for fault in herself that she plain never noticed fault in anybody else. She'd walk through fire before hurting anyone's feelings, that girl. The name's Harold Wilson."

Sam blinked, then shot out his hand to meet the sheriff's handshake.

"Glad we had this little talk," the sheriff said amiably. "Myself, I believe a little straight talk can avert a lot of trouble. And some people in my town—one in particular—has had all the trouble that she can take. If you get my drift?"

"I get your drift, and I appreciate your taking the time to talk with me, and though you may not believe it, we're on the same posse."

The sheriff didn't linger after that. Long after the patrol car disappeared from sight, Sam stood motionless, reflecting on the whole conversation. Wilson had arranged to check him out, he realized. Between Linc and the local law, Valentine had an unusual pair of protectors. Sam liked them both.

More relevant, the sheriff had helped fill in some of the puzzle pieces. Not all. But enough.

He knew what he was going to do now.

It was past nine when Val arrived home from the store. Linc, the sweetie, had thoughtfully left on the porch light for her, but more rare of him, he'd forgotten to lock the front door. Val dropped the unneeded key back into her purse, walked in and abruptly discovered another surprise. She sniffed. The faint, fragrant scent of smoke in the air was unmistakable.

Throwing down her purse, she pedaled in a half-dozen steps. Panic at the idea of a fire immediately disappeared. The glass doors to her Florida room were slid open. Just outside, she found the source of the smoke. Clouds of it were enthusiastically billowing from a charcoal fire in the barbecue grill, next to which was a platter heaped with two monster-sized steaks.

The view struck her as amazing, considering that she didn't own a grill, had never owned a grill, and her freezer hadn't stocked steaks in the past two calendar years.

Cautiously she crossed the living room and hall toward the kitchen. More miracles. Darling, her Red Cross dummy, was nowhere in sight, and her church music had disappeared. Two places were set at the table. A bottle of nonalcoholic wine lay in a chilled icer. A fresh-tossed salad lay in the crystal bowl she usually kept on the top cupboard shelf. Lit, center table, were two tall vanilla-scented candles that she could have sworn were in her bedroom that morning. A single yellow daffodil, impossibly out of season, rested on her plate.

And a man hovered over her stove in cuffed shirt-sleeves, a kitchen towel hanging out of a jeans pocket, with a spoon in one hand and a package of frozen broccoli in the other. The same man who was supposed to be on his way to Chicago. The same man who'd promised her he was going to be on his way to Chicago.

"Hi, honey."

So innocent. The gentle, mellow tenor. The boyish yank of hair on his brow, the clean-cut bones, the beguilingly open and honest brown eyes. It was a face that little old ladies would trust in a crowd, a voice no child could be afraid of.

Val knew better.

With a sinking sensation she leaned weakly against the doorjamb. It was the kiss, she thought dismally. Somehow he'd taken that kiss as an invitation to stay. And if she'd just *known* he was going to kiss her in the bookstore, she'd have frozen up like an iceberg. But Sam had sneaked that damned kiss before she could think. Now he probably thought she cared about him. He probably thought she'd been wildly glad to be in his arms, that his touch made her feel shivery all over, that no man had ever made her feel as…soft…as Sam did.

Which was all true. And Val was used to making mistakes, terrible, irrevocable mistakes, but letting Sam guess how she felt rated worse than inexcusable.

"Shepherd." She tried to project aggravation in her voice. "You told me you were leaving. You promised. You swore—"

"And I *am* still leaving, sweetheart. Just not quite yet. The truth is that I'm kind of stuck here for a few days. I need to get the steaks on. Why don't you kick off your shoes and relax for a few minutes."

With a potential tornado in her life, a woman was not inclined to *relax*. Val trailed his footsteps out to the grill. When he forked on the thick T-bones, the charcoal was still flaming. Either Sam didn't know how to cook or he liked his steaks ruined—the surface seared while the inside was still rare. It was the unhealthiest of all possible ways to cook red meat and he couldn't know, she promised herself, that she loved it that way. "*Why* are you stuck here for a few days?" she asked patiently.

He looked up with a grin, as if he'd hoped she would ask. "Because of my sister-in-law, Regan. See, she's in Chicago with my brother—Cole's minding the air freight business while I'm gone. We were partners until they got married. Then I bought him out, which suited everybody because they wanted to settle in the Southwest. But the point is that Regan flew to Chicago with him so I could take this mini-vacation. She's from Chicago, has a hundred friends there she hadn't seen in an age. And she's as close to a sister as I've got. If I cut short her time there by showing up back home too soon, she'll be disappointed. I *have* to stay for at least a few more days."

"That explanation is so convoluted that it almost sounds true. Almost."

"So suspicious." Sam passed by her with the platter of steaks, close enough to violently arouse her salivary glands. They were perfectly burned. "If you want, I can show you pictures of Regan and Cole from my wallet."

Val didn't doubt he had a brother and a sister-in-law. She doubted his intentions in the classic sense of the word. Sam could outcharm and outtalk a politician, but at core, she'd always sensed that he wasn't as easygoing as he let on. He made it sound as if all he wanted was to spend a few days with a friend. Which was fine. Only their playful friendship had always edged toward serious feelings, and potentially hurting a good man—maybe the best man she'd ever known—was not a risk Val was willing to take.

At dinner, though, he served garlic bread. Her natural caution slipped a notch. What man with sexual pursuit on his mind would serve garlic bread? And over the rare treat of a steak, her worries eased another notch. All Sam did was talk. About their experience in the Gulf, about their mutual discouragement in Middle East politics since, about feeling like tiny cogs in a huge bewildering wheel. He told her about losing his family, about how long it had taken him to get his life back on track, about why and how he'd become a pilot and what it meant to him.

They'd talked before, shared a natural easiness, but Sam hadn't opened up about himself before, not as one friend to another. He didn't make a single innuendo. Didn't once look at her as if desire were on his mind. Initially her defensive instincts were alerted when he shut off the kitchen lights and the only illumination between them was the romantic double flame from the vanilla candles. By candlelight, the strong masculine lines of Sam's face were highlighted. At a certain angle, his eyes looked darker than ebony, unfathomable as moonlight... worrisome.

But long before the end of the meal, Val had figured out why he'd chosen to eat by candlelight, and it had nothing to do with creating a romantic ambience. "Sam... did you think if we ate in the dark that I wouldn't notice?"

"Notice what?"

"I saw the contents of the refrigerator when you took out the butter," she said patiently. "I owe you a giant thanks. I knew I was running low on groceries but I was too busy to shop. What was the bill?"

Sam poured her a second glass of nonalcoholic wine. "It's my fault. I didn't mean to buy so much.

The thing was that Lincoln wasn't going to let me in the house, and I was trying to make friends with the kid, so I took him for a drive. I was only going to get tonight's meal from the grocery store—I was hardly going to mooch off you, Red. But Linc, he was having so much fun filling up the cart that I didn't have the heart to stop him. He's one special kid."

"I think so, too. His mother had a heck of a time after her husband split, but she's getting it financially back together now. Linc just got temporarily lost between the cracks. All he needed was someone to trust him, to take the time to *value* him...." Abruptly Val frowned. Sam looked willing to discuss her young friend all night. A most effective distraction. "But back to the point. What was the amount of that grocery bill?"

"Lincoln has it. I'll get it from him and let you know tomorrow." Sam whisked a slab of devil's food cake in front of her. Mounded with whipped-cream frosting. She couldn't imagine where he'd been hiding it. "In the meantime, I want to talk about something else. The ocean. I've flown over it I don't know how many times, but I've never had the chance to see it up close, and your store's closed on Sunday. Think you could spare a couple hours and take a drive to the coast with me?"

"Am I going to have the bill for those groceries by Sunday?"

"Sure, you are," Sam agreed promptly.

"And are you really only planning on being here just a few more days?"

"Only a very few more days," Sam confirmed.

Her guard was down. Her defenses darn near destroyed. But something flickered in his eyes, something more than candlelight, something that assaulted every annoying feminine hormone in her body with melting softness. And Val had made mistakes before. Mistake-making was her specialty. She couldn't, wouldn't, refused to, take any risk of hurting Sam.

"Shepherd." She looked at him straight over the damnably seductive flames. "If you're lying to me, I'll never trust you again. Maybe I wasn't totally honest with you before, but I'm being honest now. I'm in a little trouble. You've been in town long enough to have figured that out by now. I admit it, but it's trouble that I have to handle on my own. And I need to do that my own way."

"I understand," Sam agreed.

But that flicker was in his eyes again. That flicker that tended to toast her body temperature and make her toes curl. So she laid it out for him, just so neither one of them could conceivably have any illusions about flickers or anything else. "I have a store that's going bankrupt. I'm burning the candles at both ends. I'm living the life of a celibate monk and I'm as popular in this town as poison ivy. Trust me, Shepherd. I am *not* a woman you need to be involved with."

"Are you leading this conversation anywhere in particular, honey?"

"Yes. I'll take you to the ocean, and I'll spend what time with you that I can over the next few days. But..." She took a breath. Beneath the table her knees were locked together like glue. Sam didn't seem to realize that this level of honesty was difficult for her. Even so, her voice came out cracked. "But I won't sleep with you, Sam. I mean it. It's friends or it's nothing. And that's that."

"Okay," Sam said.

Five

The soccer ball arced high and plopped at the edge of a sand dune. Val scrambled up the rise and repositioned herself behind the ball. The black-and-white missile soared straight toward him. "Get out of my way, you big galoot. I'm coming in for a goal and nobody's gonna stop me."

Since no one else was on the deserted beach, Sam assumed he was the galoot in question. So far, his job of guarding the goal had been less than taxing. This time her kick sent the soccer ball spinning sideways, where it plunked into the ocean shallows and sprayed salt water in every direction. A wave sucked the ball into deeper water and Val splashed in after it.

She scooped up the ball with her hands. What Valentine knew about the game of soccer would fit in a thimble, but Sam didn't care.

It was more than an hour's drive to the coast, and they'd had a late start. So late that a fat red globe of a sun perched over the dunes to the west, ready to drop any minute now. The sand had a golden crust in the evening light, and the Atlantic Ocean was gradually lapping up more shoreline with every frothy, silvery wave. Gulls squawked and screamed, fishing for their dinner. Higher up the beach, houses hid behind tall breakwaters, but Sam hadn't seen another soul since they arrived.

That suited him fine. He wanted Val alone. He'd hoped for the whole day with her, but that proved impossible. Val started off her Sunday mornings in church, where the pastor had told him she was the only organist around. After church, she regularly volunteered a couple of hours at the hospital. No one in town, Sam noticed, was against using Valentine's talents or free time. But he hadn't heard any thank-yous, and he hadn't seen anyone pausing to chat. It had damn near killed him, watching them snub her.

Soon he intended to tackle that problem, but not now, not yet. Tonight, the only thing he wanted to tackle was Val.

She'd been dressed all day in a subdued print dress with a lace collar and old-lady shoes. Thankfully she'd jettisoned that getup before the drive, but her mood hadn't loosened up until he brought out the soccer ball.

Her mood was plenty loose now, and her appearance delectably close to destroyed. The deepening blue sky was behind her, and the hair that bounced down her back was the color of cinnamon on fire. Her feet were crusted with sand and sea salt, and her legs were bare. Too bare. Somewhere beneath a voluminous green T-shirt, Sam knew darn well she was wearing shorts. His hormones might be more subdueable if he could physically see those shorts instead of all that leg.

Maybe not. The hellion pelting toward him had a bloodthirsty gleam in her eyes. She zigged. She zagged. And then she zipped straight past his defensive crouch, her legs spinning toward the gray log of driftwood they were calling a goal.

She zoomed past the driftwood and tossed down the ball. "Hot dog. Touchdown!" she crowed. "I told you I could beat you at this, didn't I? Didn't I?"

"You did." Sam wasn't about to tell her that no one gave credit for touchdowns in soccer. Who cared? She was having fun. In the past few days, Sam had developed a disturbing picture of the burdens Val was trying to tote alone, and it had taken all his energies to coax her to relax with him. She was slow to convince that he didn't give a serious damn. That he wasn't going to put any moves on her. That he simply wanted to share a little vacation time with a friend.

At the moment Sam couldn't imagine a lie he wouldn't willingly tell her—not when the wages of sin were so worthwhile.

She scooped up the ball and perched it on her hip in a classic feminine pose of a woman begging for trouble. Those eyes. A gold-tipped hazel, full of sexy sass, just goading him to take her on. "You're probably way too tired for a rematch."

"In your dreams."

"Good heavens, you actually want another beating? You're sure your masculine ego could take it?"

"Red?"

"Yeah?"

"Kick the ball."

She did. Straight over the crest of a dune. It took all his cheating skills to insure she won. Two goals later, Sam hooked an arm around her neck and begged for mercy, or at least for a cola from the cooler so *he* had a chance to cool down.

The cooler was in the car's back seat. He flipped the tops on two cans and handed her one. Val's cheeks were flushed, tendrils of hair curling damply on her temples as she guzzled half her cola and finally caught her breath. By then the sky had softened from sunset reds to purples to the hazy deep blue of a beckoning night. The gulls had stopped screaming. Even the ocean seemed to have quieted down, content to lap silvery pools of foam at the shore.

But Valentine wasn't ready to settle down yet. Her thirst was quenched, but not her energy level. She pranced back to the shore with her arms flung wide. "You haven't said. Do you like my ocean?"

He started to grin. "Own the whole thing, do you?"

"Sure do. Claimed it when I was six years old. Decided the whole thing was mine, because no one else could love it as much as I did."

He fell into step beside her, drawn to the water's edge, watching her play barefoot tag with the waves. "In Chicago, at night, lots of nights, I'll drive to the lake. And then just walk. I'm willing to admit that Lake Michigan might be spit small next to this, but it's still water as far as you can see. At night you can't tell where the water ends and the sky begins."

Her face lifted to his. "You understand."

"I understand loneliness." He picked up a shell, tossed it into the waves. "Is that why you married him, Red?"

If he'd asked such a personal question even days before, she would have evaded it with the subtle skill of an escape artist—especially a question about the jerk. Now she just looked at him, then glanced away. "I married him for the obvious reason. I thought I was in love with him."

"And were you?"

"Yes." She hesitated. "No." She shoved her hands into the pockets of her white shorts. "He hardly turned out to be perfect, but there was a time I thought he was. That's what first drew me. Ron...he didn't get flat tires. Never put his foot in his mouth. Never wore the wrong clothes. I thought some of that perfection of his might rub off. He fit in my family better than I did, always seemed to know the right thing to do."

Sam watched her squish her toes in a wet sandy hole. A wave rode in and bubbled around her ankles. "Those things were important to you?"

"Very much. I had a notoriously long history of making mistakes. Impulsive, thoughtless mistakes." She lifted her head with a wry, dry grin. "And in this town, because I was the last in the line of Shroeders, I couldn't get gum on my shoes without someone noticing. I was always caught. Even for the most innocent pranks."

"Your parents?"

"They were older when they had me. Mom was over forty. Both of them invested an enormous amount of time, love, attention. Dad was reading me classics when I was four. Mom had me in ballet, art classes. Darned if I know why none of it took. I have this vague memory of climbing down the rose trellis from the second-story balcony...I had to be about seven.

Broke my leg. It was one of the nights the senator was over to dinner.''

"Whoops."

"If I haven't made it clear before, my life's been full of those whoops, Sam. My parents stuck by through the mess with Ron. They've always stuck by me. But I'm pretty sure they must have wondered, years ago, if their baby hadn't been switched with someone else's in the delivery room."

She smiled, inviting him to share the humor.

Sam didn't see much humor involved. The sheriff had helped him understand that neither the floundering store nor the scandal with the jerk were the real problems taking Val down. It was that habit of hers— an old, old habit—of thinking of herself as a disgrace, a disappointment.

For a long time his redhead had been deluded into seeing herself as unlovable. But breaking the habit, Sam thought, was going to be a tad tricky. Particularly when the woman in question was as hardheaded as a brick wall. And as vulnerable as the drop of dew on a petal-soft rose. And that petal-soft smile of hers abruptly froze.

"*What* do you think you're doing, Shepherd?"

"It's late. You have to work tomorrow, and we still have a long drive home." Sam peeled off his sweatshirt and dropped it in the sand. "But I can't come all this way to the ocean without a swim."

"The *last* thing you want is a swim. It's November, you nut. Don't be fooled because we've been having some warm days. If you wade in more than a few feet, the water'll be colder than ice—"

"You'd better not come in then. I promise I won't be long."

Her voice was beginning to rise. "You don't know the ocean. You don't know about jellyfish and sting-rays and drop-offs and currents. This is nothing like swimming in a lake, Sam, and when it's this pitch-dark—holy kamoly, you put those jeans back on!"

"Now, Valentine. You've seen a man's bare behind before."

"I don't give a sweet daisy about your bare behind! I'm telling you it's not safe to swim! Tarnation, Shepherd—"

She splashed out after him, mad enough to spit but, more relevant to Sam, endearingly determined to save him from a potential drowning. And she was right, he discovered. Splashing around the shallows, the water temperature was misleadingly mild. Just past, even no deeper than knee level, the temperature dropped like a stone. Not that it mattered. He'd never planned on swimming anyway.

Valentine clearly wasn't expecting him to suddenly turn. She ran smack-dab into his bare chest. Instinctively she clutched his shoulders for balance. Seconds later, she was still holding on tight, but for different reasons entirely.

His palms cradled the sides of her head and he took her mouth. Hard. Not like a friend would kiss her. Not like that milksop perfectionist of a con artist she'd married. And not, Sam suspected, like she wanted to be kissed. Passion obviously wasn't high on Val's wish list; she'd already married once on a classic if mis-guided quest of security, stability and respectability.

Sam didn't want her forming illusions that she was going to find any of that nonsense with him. He didn't give a damn about respectability, and stability was the last thing he wanted her to feel in his arms.

Initially his bareness unnerved her... but then she seemed to forget those other priorities. In the moonlight he saw her eyes turn liquid and luminous. She liked those long, drugging kisses. She liked the slow, exploring sweep of his tongue, the feel of his hands swallowed in the weight of her hair, the earthy rub of his whiskered cheek against her throat.

Her hands slipped from his shoulders, encountered his chest. A wave broke, splashing around her knees; she didn't seem to notice. At first tentative and shy, then more boldly, her fingers furled his chest hair against the grain, testing the heat and heartbeat just beneath the muscled skin. A drop of salt water on his shoulder seemed to mesmerize her. Then, with a kitten's curiosity, she leaned forward to lick it off.

And Valentine was so sure there wasn't a trace of hellion left in her.

Sam pulled her out of the waves and sank with her onto the sand, kissing her even as he was covering her. She'd been like this in the Gulf. Rapunzel undone when she let down her hair. Beauty unafraid of the Beast. He'd never guessed she'd been married. She came on, to him, with him, like an untried princess disarmed to discover that an earthy sensuality was as natural to her as breathing. She made him feel as though he was her first man, her only man, as if he could do absolutely anything when he was with her.

All he wanted to do, at this precise moment, was make her feel loved. The need drove him beyond passion, although this close to Val, electricity thrummed through his pulse with the heat and volatility of a hot wire. Lying length to length, desire soared and then sharpened like the honed edge of a blade. He ignored it. He'd heard all he could stand about the terrible mistakes she'd made and the dreadful flaws in her character and the worst, this foolish illusion she had about being a disappointment.

He was gonna make Val feel loved or die trying.

His touch reverent and praising, he stroked the soft swell of her breast above her T-shirt, warming his hands, warming her, before reaching under the fabric. She made a sound, a fretful sound, when his palm cupped the small mound of her breast. Knowing Val, she probably found fault with her body, too, so he meticulously, tenderly, communicated how exquisite he found her right breast. And then her left. The pale hollow in between, he stroked with his tongue. She was precious to him, treasured beyond price, infinitely worth loving. He told her with his touch and tongue, soothing her, cherishing her, showing her how beautiful she was in every way he could think of. Her nipples, though, were extraordinarily sensitive. Possibly unbearably sensitive, because as gentle as he was, Val made another sound—a feline sound of pure frustration—and suddenly wrapped around him closer than butter on bread.

It seemed he was getting through. At least for that moment, Valentine definitely wasn't worried about being a disappointment.

She claimed an openmouthed kiss, his hellion, that was hot enough to bake the night-cooled sand.

After that, he nearly lost it. They rolled like kids in the sand, only neither was playing. Val matched caress for caress, kiss for kiss, pleated on top of him one minute, glued beneath him the next. Her beautiful hair was tangled in sand and salt and shot with pale moonlight. The chemical components of the earth's atmosphere never had, never could, scientifically include longing. But it was longing he tasted in her kisses, longing she communicated to him in her touch.

Beyond the roar of ocean, there was no sound but for his rough breathing, hers. Sam was losing all control. And knew it. When he pressed her, snuggling tight, against his thighs, he was hard enough to bore rock. She could have shied away then. She should have shied away then. His eyes burned from wanting. For her. She had to know it was for her, and this wasn't like in the Gulf, when she'd been secure in the knowledge that nothing could go too far.

Only she didn't shy away. She rubbed against him, yielding, asking, until the only thought in his head was peeling off the bitsy scrap of white shorts and taking her. She wanted him. Then, there, now. Claws of need blurred his conscience. He already knew that her intense, wild responsiveness was hardly proof that she loved him, but he didn't care. She needed and wanted. He could build on that. The most primitive man understood the value of staking a claim. He wanted the rights of a lover: the right to protect her, to work with her fears and lack of confidence from the inside, the right to be part of her life.

But damnation, there were freezing little waves swirling at their feet, the sand was less than a desirable mattress and the open beach far too exposed. It just wasn't the right time and place, not for a redhead who was already prone to see herself as making impulsive mistakes.

Sam didn't want her believing the first time they made love was no more than a vulnerable impulse.

And he sure as hell didn't want to give her any excuse to think of him as a *mistake*.

He kissed her again, because there was no way on earth he could deprive himself of one last kiss, and then inhaled a lungful of oxygen and rolled a foot away. The sky was velvet, dusted with benevolent twinkling stars. Pretty, but they. didn't do a damn thing to quench the fire. The cool night air feathering over his skin was just as worthless. Wanting her wasn't going to go away by wishing it.

He turned his head. Val had flopped over on her stomach, using her crossed arms as a pillow, and he couldn't see her face beyond the rumpled curtain of hair. When he had his heartbeat under control, he reached over and gently lifted a bedraggled strand for a peek. Somewhere from that nest of white arms and shadowed cheeks came a voice.

"Something...unfortunate...seems to happen when I'm around you, Shepherd."

He heard the wobbly attempt at humor. Humor, in the Gulf, had always been Valentine's first line of defense. "I wouldn't call it unfortunate," he murmured.

"Well, I'd call it shameful. Not on your part. You were lonely. I knew you were lonely in the Gulf, and it's no crime to reach out. But God, I can't *stand* a woman who says no and then acts like yes. Dammit, Sam. I'm not a tease."

He noticed, not for the first time, how brilliantly she managed to excuse him and take all blame for any potential wrong on herself. "Personally, I don't think what happened had anything to do with either teasing or loneliness. I'd say it had more to do with the natural meeting of a match and nitroglycerin."

"But that's the point. That chemistry springing out of nowhere. I thought—I *believed*—that we were doing a good job being friends."

"We *are* friends." Slowly he dragged her up to a sitting position and scraped back her wild mane of hair so he could see her face. Her skin was as pale as moonlight, her lips still damp, still soft from his kisses. But her eyes met his, wet and luminous and so, so wary. Quietly he asked her, "Do you trust me?"

"Sam," she said patiently, "try and see this from my point of view. I'm not *supposed* to trust you. I *can't* trust you. It's my job as a human being to notice that I've made a confused mess of my life—especially concerning my judgment about men—and to have the good sense to learn some caution. Gullible is not cute. I've got a rule book at home that says I'm not supposed to believe what a man tells me just because I happen to like him."

She was trying to make him smile, but that puckish humor of hers never reached her eyes. He gently brushed a strand of hair from her cheek. "I agree. It wouldn't hurt you to get tougher about men. I don't want you to trust the other guys. I just want to know if you trust me."

Val took another long, patient breath. "You haven't given me a single reason to. You've been in town how many days? You've gotten me drunk. You've lied to me. You involved an innocent nine-year-old boy in a conspiracy to forget the price of those damn groceries. I've told you how things are, how I really feel, and you seem to agree, and the next thing I know we're rolling in the sand. In broad moonlight. Risking a potential charge for indecent exposure."

"Honey, get to the point."

She rolled her eyes to the white sliver of a moon. "The point is that *maybe* I trust you, Sam. *Maybe*. An eensy-teensy bit—no more."

Sam understood that her admission of trust had been a major risk for Valentine.

Which made it particularly tough to willingly and deliberately betray her.

Faces appeared in shop windows as he ambled down the business zone on the main street. He'd purposefully developed a daily pattern. First he bought a paper at the drugstore, then picked up something for breakfast at the bakery, then wandered into the post office. Occasionally he made other stops, but those were the ones that mattered. All three places were managed by women who'd been financially hurt by Val's ex, and all three women fed the negative gossip mill about Val.

"You're still in town," June Shraver said as she handed him change for his newspaper.

"It seems I've grown attached to your Chekapee."

"I haven't seen you with Valerie Shroeder in almost a week. I guess you saw for yourself what she was, didn't you?"

"I sure did," Sam said feelingly.

Outside, the morning was chipper and brisk. Whistling weather. He passed by Val's bookstore without pausing. Later he'd see her, as he'd seen her every day. But not in the store and not in town. Val wanted it that way—she didn't want him suffering any repercussions from being associated with the town pariah. But Sam had to admit, their evening excursions away from town served a dual purpose. The gossips believed that he'd jumped on their bandwagon and had cut all ties with Val.

Temporarily, that was exactly what Sam wanted them to believe.

Martha Witherspoon predictably spotted him through the bakery window. When he walked in, the elderly woman was already forking a still-warm doughnut onto a slice of waxed paper. "Coffee, Mr. Shepherd?"

"You'd be saving my life," he admitted shyly. Heaven knows, Martha had been trying to "save him," from his first doughnut in her store. Sam gathered early on that the dangers of the damned were nothing compared to the risk of involvement with one Valerie Shroeder. Martha's tale-telling this morning went back fifteen years, to a pajama party during which Valentine had had the very bad judgment to put food colouring into Ms. Witherspoon's granddaughter's shampoo. "Blue," Martha said morosely. "Blue food coloring. You have no idea what my granddaughter went through to get it out."

"I can imagine," Sam said sympathetically.

"I'm telling you, Mr. Shepherd, that girl was never up to any good. And she's even more brazen than she used to be. Still attending church, still helping out at the hospital . . . as if she thought we'd trust her now, after all she's done. Why, I could tell you stories . . . ."

"Tell me." Sam leaned on the counter like a fellow conspirator.

He didn't hear anything new. The recycled childhood tales always painted his darling as an irrepressible scamp—God, he wished he'd known her then. But the tales never justified his Valentine being crucified. Whenever serious hard feelings came up, Ron's name was mentioned in the same breath. Val was just a scapegoat for the real jerk who'd hurt them.

He left the bakery a half hour later, with his hands slugged in his pockets and his jaw set. He'd listened for days, like a soldier accumulating ammunition for a siege. Now he was ready to put the siege in motion. Breaking his usual pattern, he aimed west. One of the local realtors was his goal, and his visit there he hoped was going to put a little bomb under the town of Chekapee. They were all so sure they wanted to get back at Val.

Sam was about to give him the ideal chance.

He crossed the street against the red light, paying no attention to traffic. From the first day, he knew he had to do something about the way the townspeople were treating Val. What he'd prefer to do was kick some behinds. However imminently satisfying that option, it didn't solve the problem. You could tell people they were wrong from here to China. Unless they saw it for themselves, nothing got changed.

There was an old adage about fighting fire with fire. And the strategy of a plan had taken root, for Sam, when he realized the parallel potential of the situation. He was from the North. So was the jerk Val had married. The women in town easily talked to him, probably because they'd judged his wholesome looks as trustworthy. Ron, also, had wholesome looks. The townspeople all seemed to like him. Once upon a time, they'd all liked Rat Bait, too.

Most relevant, the jerk had taken Valentine for a rough ride. And if Sam was infinitely careful, he could make it seem as if he were taking her in just as ruthlessly as her ex had.

He knocked at the realtor's door, then stepped in. Rose Wilkins promptly rose from behind a scarred-veneer desk. She looked like he'd expected—a bottle blond with a sway in her behind and a heavy hand with a mascara wand—and from the gossip mill, Sam already knew that her daddy's considerable savings had been lost in the banking debacle. The "girls" claimed she'd been consoling herself with men ever since. From the avid way she looked him over, Sam could believe it.

He made it quickly clear that he was a serious potential customer. "There's an empty storefront on River, with a sign For Rent in front. I wonder if you could tell me what the terms are."

The predator gleam in her eyes didn't disappear, only changed. She crossed around the desk to offer a handshake, her gaze still hungry but in a completely different way. "It's valuable property." She hesitated. The amount of rental fee she'd named clearly worried her. "Of course, we strongly want to encourage new business in Chekapee. Possibly that rate is negotiable if I really thought you were serious."

"Oh, I'm serious. I'm real taken with your town, and I've had some investment money burning a hole in my pocket for a chance to do something with it. But I don't want a year's lease."

"I'm sorry. It's only available on an annual lease."

"Okay. Thanks for your trouble." Sam rapped his knuckles on her desk and turned to leave.

"Wait." The potential fish was leaving. Her voice reached a high soprano of panic before leveling down. "Exactly what terms did you want?"

Sam wouldn't be here if he hadn't done his homework. The property in question had been vacant for a long, lonely, expensive year. But he shrugged his shoulders as if this were all new to him. "I wouldn't mind an option for a full year, but all I want to be pinned down to is three months. I figured that three months would give me enough time to see if my business was going to make it."

He could almost see the wheels clicking in her head. The fish on the hook wasn't the fat marlin she'd dreamed of, but a fish was still a fish. "What business did you have in mind?"

"I want to open a bookstore."

She stared at him as if he'd lost his mind. "Possibly you didn't notice that just five doors down and across the street, there's already a bookstore. The Book Nook. Valerie Shroeder's—"

"I know." Sam waited a moment to let that sink in. "It was my impression," he said carefully, "that no one in town would mind if she had a little competition."

"Competition," the woman echoed. Silence, then a slow bloodthirsty light dawned in her pale brown eyes. "Another bookstore would put her out of business. Good and out," she murmured, and then looked up at him. "My family had everything in the bank, every cent my father had ever put away. It's gone now. Might as well have burned it in a bonfire."

"I've heard the story," Sam said.

"If you've been in town long, you must have heard it was *her* husband who was responsible."

"I heard. I had the feeling Ms. Shroeder wasn't too well liked. In fact, if she did all the things I've heard her accused of..." Sam shook his head disgustedly, silently communicating that all his allegiance was with the town—and nowhere near the lady he loved. "I mean...you all *trusted* her." He added musingly, "I'll bet it would feel good to watch *her* trust someone, and have him shaft her high and dry. It'd serve her right if some guy really took her for a ride, wouldn't it?"

"Lord, it sure would." The realtor abruptly straightened. "We'll go with a three-month lease. Although I have to confess, I hardly think that's a reasonably fair time for you to get in and renovate and even get started—"

"That's not a problem," Sam informed her. "I plan to open the bookstore within a week."

"A week?"

"A week."

"A *week?*" she repeated again.

Sam smiled. "Trust me, I have all the business connections to make it possible, and I'm in a hurry to make this happen. The only thing that could possibly slow me up is the time it'll take you to put the paperwork together."

Less than an hour later, he had a key and a promise that he'd have more help "than he knew what to do with." When he left the office, Rose Wilkins was already reaching for the telephone.

Sam felt like the soldier who'd fired the first shot in a war. There was no going back now. As he walked down River Street, his stomach was pitching enough acid to make him feel ill. He never liked fooling people. He liked even less playing the role of a manipulative bastard like Val's ex.

Drastic problems required drastic solutions, Sam told himself. If the plan he'd set in motion was outrageous, he'd needed something fast—and shocking—to wake up Valentine's sleepy little town. To sit around and watch his redhead being hurt was untenable. He'd had to take action.

But in a week, if not sooner, Val was going to discover what he'd done.

She wasn't gonna like it.

Most guys came courting with candy and flowers, Sam thought glumly. In the whole history of man, he couldn't think of a single lover who'd tried to win and woo his lady by criminal tactics that were ultimately going to include lying, breaking into buildings and outright thievery.

But most women didn't have the shell of fear around their hearts that his Valentine did.

Unless he did something drastic and desperate enough to dent that shell, Sam was painfully aware that he had no chance—none—of winning her.

Six

As bad days went, this one had been a Gorgon. Another distributor had threatened to cut her off, her latest discount promotion had failed to bring in new faces, and her clutch of loyal customers simply wasn't enough to stop the tide of bills. Jonesey came in early, claimed she looked more beat than a whipped dog and ordered her home. As Val gathered up her purse and sweater and headed for the back door of the store, her mood was broody and crabby and flat-out discouraged. Until she pushed open the door and saw the car blocking the alley.

The passenger door of the white Mustang was already hanging open, begging for a hitchhiker. Its driver—a gentleman with caramel brown eyes and a crooked grin just full of hell—cupped his finger. And her heavy heart, that quickly started thumping as maniacally as a puppy's tail. With a smile and a chuckle, she threw her sweater and purse in back and climbed in.

"I'll have you know I don't go off with just any good-looking man who tries to pick me up, Shepherd. You're the only exception."

"All the girls tell me that."

She laughed as she strapped in. "I didn't expect to see you until after nine. You couldn't have known I was getting off early—"

"I didn't know. I saw Jonesey walking into the store, and thought I'd take the chance." Sam's gaze roved over her lace-trimmed blouse and long print skirt, then focused on her face. "Rough day?"

She promptly and cheerfully denied it, but Sam—so typically—drew his own conclusions. Within minutes the wind was whipping through her hair and the car tooling down a quiet stretch of black highway. As if he knew she hadn't taken time for lunch, a white bag of fast food appeared in her lap. Dire consequences were threatened if she failed to level it. While she dutifully munched, Sam pushed in an old rock-and-roll tape with a lot of mindlessly silly do-be-do's and wah-wah-wah's, turned the volume on high and demanded, the bully, that she kick off her shoes.

Stress didn't stand a prayer of a chance. Not with Sam, she mused. It wasn't that her problems disappeared, but when she was with him, nothing else seemed half as important. As the miles peeled by, she leaned back her head and simply savored the night, the wind, the speed . . . and the dangerous magic of Mr. Carson Sam Shepherd.

They'd spent every evening together for more than a week. And every evening she'd felt the sweet, dark feminine pull—a sexual awareness of him that she couldn't shake, an emotional draw for him that kept growing, as hopeless as a cure for the flu, the more she was with him.

But there had been no more passes from Sam. No kisses, now touches, no explosive fires started like that night on the beach.

He'd finally accepted that she was only interested in friendship, Val thought with relief. And the chemistry would fade for her in time. It had to. Her pattern of disappointing people she loved had yet to be broken. Judging from her store, she had another failure in the making. Sam didn't need a lover that he was ashamed of. She couldn't, wouldn't, risk hurting him that way, but there was so much risk with a friendship, especially a friendship based on honesty and trust.

And Sam, in a dozen ways, had proved his willingness to be totally and completely honest with her.

"We're nearly to the coast," she remarked when she noticed the passing highway signs.

"Close enough to smell the ocean, but we're not going to the beach itself. A few days ago when I was driving, I discovered a place that I wanted you to see. We'll be there in two shakes." Once she'd demolished the fast food, he produced an apple. Shepherd was big on her daily quota of vitamin C.

"Sam?" Her teeth crunched into the shiny red skin. "You haven't said a word about going back to Chicago, but I know you can't stay forever. You've already been here longer than you planned." Even thinking about his heading north made her feel a spear of loss, but the question had to be asked. "It won't hurt you, your business, extending your vacation like this?"

"According to my brother—and I've talked on the phone with Cole every day—they're thriving without me. My setup's pretty small, Valentine. Occasionally we air-freight something exciting, but most of the time we're making regular runs for established customers. There's nothing my brother doesn't know, and for the rest of the staff—there's a mechanic, a couple other pilots, Georgia mans the office...everyone knows what they're doing. I doubt they even miss me."

Val noted the almost imperceptible change in his voice when he mentioned Georgia. It had happened before. "Your brother isn't too inconvenienced by your being gone this long?"

"Hell, no." Sam shot her a grin. "There isn't much going on in Cripple Creek in November but snow. He's missed flying, so this is more fun for him than work. And I've talked to Cole's wife, Regan, three times. She's managed to stuff my brother in a suit and is having a ball, showing him the romantic spots in Chicago. She claims I'm going to have a niece or nephew out of this if I'll just stay out of their hair a while longer."

Val finished off the apple. She loved hearing Sam talk about Cole. Although the brothers had been through grief and hard times, it was obvious they'd come together as a close family of two, which told her a great deal about Sam's feelings on love and loyalty. "You're really fond of your sister-in-law, aren't you?"

"You bet. Regan's perfect for him. She looks like an angel—blond hair, big green eyes—but she's full of pepper and life. My brother developed a pretty tough edge after our parents died. I used to worry that he wouldn't find a woman smart enough—and caring enough—to see past it. Regan is one terrific lady."

"And is Georgia terrific, too?"

"Georgia?"

Val neatly wrapped up the apple core in a napkin. "You've mentioned her a few times. She's the woman who answers your phone, mans your office, handles your bookkeeping. And I hear the change in your voice every time her name comes up. So...she was important to you. Like you were sleeping with her?"

"How come she never told me she was nosier than a cat?" Sam asked the windshield plaintively.

She grinned. "Hey, you don't have to answer. You're the one who said you didn't want any taboo subjects between us."

"I don't. Ever." Although the road was Satan black and poorly lit, Sam took his eyes off the windshield long enough to meet her gaze. As if to prove how honest he wanted to be with her, his voice turned serious, quiet. "You were right about Georgia. Before I went to the Gulf, we were lovers. For more than a year. I think we both assumed it would work into more than a sexual relationship, and eventually became mutually uncomfortable when it didn't." He added. "She's married now, has been for six months. Actually, I introduced them."

When he braked and turned off the engine, Val didn't notice their location—or care. Disgracefully x-rated pictures had filled her mind when he first started talking about *Georgia*. The relationship had been sexually hot. Sam didn't have to put it in graphic spades, but Val's imagination did.

Momentarily she wondered—worried—whether she had what it took to satisfy him the way this Georgia had...then banished that feline lick of jealousy and nerves to a mental wastebasket.

What was the matter with her? She should have been pleased that Sam had openly told her about his past lover. She *was* pleased. Downright thrilled, in fact. No man talked about his previous love affairs—or good grief, referred to a satisfying sexual relationship—with a woman he was pursuing. Sam had quit pursuing her. They were friends. It was exactly what she wanted.

"Hey. You don't have to like the place, but somehow I thought I'd get a little different reaction than sad eyes and a big scowl."

"Pardon? Oh!" She scrambled into her shoes and then fumbled for the door latch, her gaze riveted on the view. "What a magical, wonderful place, Sam!"

The house rose three stories on a hilly section of deserted beach. It was someone's dreadfully romantic folly and built during the forties, Val suspected, because it had that aura of glamour and movie stars and extravagance. There wasn't a window left in the place; one whole wall had crumbled. Val took a step closer to the fence and caught the moonlit gleam of a sweeping white marble staircase inside.

"It's like out of a fantasy," she breathed, and then, very firmly, "We can't go in."

"I know."

"There are No Trespassing signs all over the place."

"I know."

"The whole thing looks ready to erode. Even the breakwater's gone. We're *not* going to explore."

"I know."

"I can just picture it . . . getting caught by the police for trespassing. It's the kind of thing that was always happening to me when I was a kid. And I've worked like a dog to build up a respectable reputation...." Her voice trailed off. "I'm not a kid anymore, Sam. It's been years since I did anything on impulse."

"I know." Sam cleared his throat before mentioning, "There are two high-power flashlights in the glove compartment...if for any reason you might like to know that."

Silence. And then Val pivoted on one heel and gave him a fulminating look. "If we get caught, Shepherd, I'm never going to forgive you."

They weren't going to get caught. Sam had phoned the local authorities that afternoon to ask if anyone would mind if they photographed the old ruin in the moonlight. But he had no chance to tell Val that, because she snatched the biggest flashlight and was off, ducking through a broken hole in the fence with no respect for her stockings or business clothes.

As he trailed after her, Sam admitted to himself that he wouldn't have told her anyway. The temptation was too strong to let Valentine experience that nothing terrible would happen—not with him—if she forgot that respectable, responsible nonsense and let down her hair.

And let down her hair, she did. Days before, when Sam accidentally ran across the abandoned mansion, he thought the romance of the place would appeal to Val, but now was gratified to see how much. The lines of tension and stress disappeared from her forehead. Her eyes shone with laughter and a basic, impulsive, natural joy of life. It took her a while to explore every room, but not as much time as it should have. She raced around, scaring him half to death that she was going to get hurt, the flashlight flickering up and down the staircases, accompanied by oohing and aahing at everything she discovered.

Sam thought of women who loved diamonds. And then of Valentine, whose spirit of fun was ignited by nothing more than exploring an old house. A decrepit old house. The sweeping white marble staircase was cracked, mirrored walls broken, plaster debris piled in heaps and most of the surfaces covered with sand.

"I'll be darned, Sam. There's a boudoir. You know, à la Hedy Lamarr and Gable?"

She liked the boudoir. And the butler's pantry, and the circular back staircase, and the ballroom. She nearly caused him a heart attack when she leaned over the broken banister from the second story to tell him about something else she'd found.

He ordered her down. At her own speed, she obeyed, flouncing down the white marble staircase and batting her eyelashes à la Greta Garbo.

He crooked his finger at her.

"What?"

"Just c'mere a second, Red."

"You want to fox-trot? Or hear my E. Fitzgerald – F. Sinatra combination rendition of 'Night and Day'? Or we could have a contest—who can talk as fast as Tracy and Hepburn—"

She didn't stop bubbling until he cupped his knuckles under her chin. "We can do all those things in a minute. First, I claim rights to a forfeit," Sam told her.

"A forfeit?"

"I hate to tell you this, Ms. Shroeder, but you're having fun. Plain, ordinary, innocent fun. And I'm feeling pretty good that you're having fun with me.

Are you going to have a conniption fit if I claim a kiss?''

Her skin was suddenly warm, humming warm, and the pulse in her throat thudded against his wrist. Her eyes met his, searching, wistful, yearning. At that moment Sam knew that she wanted a kiss, his kiss, and it wasn't a smooch between friends that was on her mind.

''Hey, if it's going to bother you—''

''It's all right. I don't mind, Sam,'' she whispered.

He leaned closer, until his face blocked out all the shadows, and then gently, swiftly bussed her forehead. When he immediately straightened, her eyes widened in surprise and confusion.

Sam thought they were making progress.

It didn't stop his nerves from feeling as unraveled as a loose skein of yarn. Tomorrow, Valentine would discover what he'd done. And he had no idea how she was going to react.

''I thought you told me that he was a nice guy.''

Val didn't immediately respond to Jonesey. Standing at the window with her arms wrapped around her chest, she couldn't tear her eyes away from the view across the street. Five doors down, a hairdresser had gone bankrupt more than a year before. The place had been empty ever since.

It wasn't empty now. There'd been no ads in the local newspaper announcing a new store opening, but for several days the place had buzzed and bustled with community activity. Val hadn't paid any attention. She wasn't privy to the gossip mill, and it never occurred that the action could affect her personally.

Now she realized differently. A hand-painted sign—barely legible—read Book Stall, Grand Opening. The label of *stall* was certainly appropriate, she mused, because the store had the look of a dilapidated barn. Some plywood bookshelves had been slapped together, and the rest of the stock was piled in crates. A rented cash register was set up on a card table. As far as Val could tell, no one had even bothered to remove the rusty old hair dryers from the original hair salon operation. The place was a pit...especially when compared to the lovingly welcome atmosphere of her own bookstore.

But her store was deserted.

And her new competition's doorway was jammed—literally jam-packed—with customers. As she once dreamed her own would be.

Jonesey had been sitting behind the counter, slitting bills open with the edge of a Swiss army knife. Now his teeth chomped down on an unlit stogie as he stalked around the counter to stand behind her. Jonesey still looked pale after his siege of flu, but he'd barked her head off when she'd scolded him for coming back to work last week. Bartholomew wasn't old, but he looked it. He walked with a hunch; his face was as weathered as an old leather glove, and his expression was carved in a permanent crab's scowl. He'd never been one for friends. His wife had been everything to him, and when she died, no one was close enough to offer him comfort. He made sure no one dared try.

He was wearing one of those mean-spirited taciturn scowls now. "You want I should shoot him?" he asked gruffly.

"No," Val said absently. The new Stephen King that she couldn't sell . . . he had it displayed in the dusty window, had had the nerve to jack up the jacket price a couple extra dollars and he was *still* moving it at the speed of light. Armloads. Customers were leaving his damn store with literally armloads of books.

"I thought you knew him. I thought you said he was a friend. And you had no idea he was going to do this to you?" Jonesey demanded.

"No idea at all," Val murmured. Her nerves felt like the rough side of a cat's tongue. In all this time, she'd had no idea how Sam spent the daylight hours. She'd tactfully asked him to stay away from the store. If they were seen together, someone was going to fill his ears with humiliating gossip. She'd joked about her situation but never told him how bad things really were, because she didn't want him to know, had never wanted him in the awkward position of feeling he had to defend her.

And all those evenings together, it had never occurred that Sam was hiding something from her, but just the opposite. Talking. Lord! The two of them never seemed to stop talking when they were together, whether they were eating fish and chips or boeuf bourguignonne, whether they were strolling a moon-lit beach on the coast or simply driving. Sam had told her so much about himself. He'd even told her about that damn sexy Georgia—one of a hundred things he'd done to make her believe that she could trust him, that she was getting to know the real Carson Sam Shepherd.

And then there'd been last night. In that con-demned house on the beach. They'd had such fun, and all those hours spent together had suddenly emotionally added up, for Val, the same way stray music notes, put together, finally made a song.

It was a kiss that never happened that she couldn't forget. It was the total trust she felt with Sam, the intrinsic trust that came from her heart. It was feeling the heat of his body close to hers, and knowing they were completely alone, and seeing the dark fire of desire in his eyes. It was remembering that she'd felt dangerous, and as willful as when she'd been young and stupid and vulnerable, because at that exact instant she'd have taken any risk for Sam—probably done anything he'd asked her.

He could have taken advantage. But he hadn't. With that gentle buss on her forehead, Val had understood that Sam never would, never could, take advantage of her...and that protective shell around her heart cracked. The love song she'd been trying so hard not to hear simply couldn't be denied any longer. As inevitable as rain, she realized that she was dreadfully, desperately, painfully in love with him.

Jonesey rearranged the unlit stogie to the other side of his mouth. "I heard talk about him before, but I never thought to tell you. It wasn't negative, but the opposite. The whole town thinks he's the nicest thing since apple pie—I've never seen people take to a stranger so fast. And that was nice to hear, since he was your friend. It never occurred to me that he'd stab you in the back."

"He's a sneaky low-down worm," Val murmured.

Jonesey sighed heavily. "The womenfolk. I guess you might as well know that he's especially charmed the women."

"Believe me—that's no surprise."

"He's a varmint."

"The best liar I've ever met," Val said darkly.

"And a Yankee besides." Jonesey rocked back on his wizened five-feet-four-inch frame, staring out the window with her, close but careful not to touch. Jonesey didn't like touching or being touched. All morning, though, he'd been no farther than three feet away from her unless she was using the rest room.

"What I don't understand is how he put that bookstore together so *fast*. How could he possibly have gotten the stock overnight? It doesn't make any sense. He's a flyboy. Not likely he'd have any experience or contacts with distributors and wholesalers, and *nobody* can put together a business at the drop of a hat."

Val had already puzzled out those questions. She'd also figured out the answers, which was undoubtedly why her heart was racing and her nerves more rattled than a cat's in a hurricane. She turned away from the window. She'd seen more than enough. "There's no point in talking about it anymore, Jonesey. There's nothing we can do about it this morning."

"I could still shoot him," Jonesey offered again.

"Thank you, Bartholomew, but we don't want you in trouble with the law again. If there's any murder to be done, I'll do it myself. Trust me. Mr. Carson Samuel Shepherd is not going to get away with this."

For the first time since she'd known him, Jonesey looked alarmed. "What are you going to do?"

As if it were any other work night, Val closed the bookstore at nine, drove home, grabbed a quick dinner and changed clothes.

Unlike any other night, though, she returned to the store around ten-thirty. Her normal parking place was near the rear entrance. Tonight, she parked in the deepest shadows of the alley and climbed out of the car carrying a flashlight and dressed like a thief, in black jeans and a black sweatshirt.

The dark clothes suited her mood—more relevant, they helped her blend into the night—but she hadn't anticipated the rain. When she'd left home, the sky had only been dripping. Now the heavens opened up in a Florida-style deluge, complete with cracks of lightning and thunder booms.

She couldn't waste time skulking in shadows. Racing across the alley, she fumbled in her front jeans pocket for the store key. The key fought her, partly because she couldn't see for the pouring rain and partly because she was trying so hard to make absolutely no noise.

Eventually the lock clicked, but by then rain was dripping in her eyelashes and she was shivering damp. Silent as a cat, she turned the doorknob and tiptoed in. The store was warm, thank heavens, but she'd purposefully left no security lights on that evening. The office and back room were blacker than caves. She pushed off her shoes—they were wet enough to be squeaky—and then had to wait several minutes for her eyes to adjust to the darkness. She had the flashlight but didn't want to use it unless she had to.

Barefoot, hovering in the dark, she ventured toward the main room of the store. The depth of two bookshelves in, she caught the glimpse of a wavering light. Then heard movement. Her heart started racing, and her palms dampened with nerves. She tiptoed ahead and craned her head around the edge of another bookshelf, where she saw boxes piled high at the front door—cardboard packing boxes that were chock-full of her books. The movement she'd heard, though, wasn't emanating from the front door but from behind the counter.

Her old-fashioned cash register gleamed silver in the light of a battery-powered lantern. The register drawer was gaping open, with the towering hulk of a man hunched over it.

The intruder appeared threatening enough to make any woman's heart stop. Disreputable whiskers darkened the unusually strong line of his chin. The rest of his face looked eerily white and harsh in the artificial light. Nobody'd mess with him in a dark alley—not with those huge shoulders—and Val had the brief impulse to run, fast, like mad for the back door, forget her shoes and just keep going.

But that was a coward's way out.

She switched on her flashlight and aimed it into Sam's eyes.

He froze, directly in the act of sneaking wads of money into her till. More wads of money than she'd seen in her entire months of being in business.

"Damn," he murmured. "You caught me."

Seven

"**D**on't try that innocent Boy Scout smile on me, Shepherd. You *knew* I'd figure out what you were doing!" Val still had him pinned in the flashlight and wasn't about to let him go. Maybe Sam had fooled the whole town into believing he'd stabbed her in the financial back by opening a rival bookstore, but she knew otherwise. Even the devil couldn't open a store overnight on the power of his charm alone. There was only one place on earth where he could have accumulated a source of stock that fast, and Val knew her inventory down to the last paperback. "Those were *my* books you were selling, you louse!"

"I know, honey, and the idea worked like a charm." Sam illustrated by lifting two huge fistfuls of greenbacks. "You made piles of money today."

"Forget the honey and forget the money. I've a mind to call the sheriff and have you arrested. I don't know how you got in here, but you had to either steal my store key or just plain break and enter. And then there's grand theft of my property—and from the look of those boxes near the front door, you're anticipating *more* grand theft. Not that I'm going to let you get away with this—"

"You seem to be a little ticked," Sam said cautiously.

"A *little* ticked?" Val snapped off the flashlight, wishing she *were* ticked instead of miserably sick at heart. She'd taken one look at his Grand Opening sign that morning and nearly died from guilt. Sam had conned her into believing that his feelings stopped at friendship. He'd lied. No casual *friend* went to such complicated lengths to help someone else unless he cared. Deeply and way, way too much.

She'd failed to protect everyone else she loved, but damned if she was going to hurt Sam. He had to be stopped. She'd tried being reasonable and got nowhere, but anger was a tougher weapon—and she'd had all day to work up a fake head of steam. "If you think I'm just a *little* ticked, Shepherd, you'd better be near a ground. Because if you've never seen a redhead in a full-blown temper before—"

"At least think twice before calling the sheriff, sweetheart. Honestly, I don't think it'd do you any good." Sam's tone was as soothing and easy as a balmy spring breeze. "I've met him. I really don't think he likes people in his jail. In fact, I think all he'd probably do is put me in your personal safekeeping until I shape up. Like Jonesey and Lincoln."

"You're *not* Jonesey or Lincoln." And Val didn't like it, the way he was slowly edging around the counter and coming toward her. Sam didn't appear the least intimidated by her temper. Inexplicably, he didn't even seem to notice her fake temper. His shadowed eyes had lanced on her face like a magnet that wouldn't let go. "Don't you come any closer, you low-down varmint!"

"I know you probably won't believe this, but it's a relief to hear you yelling at me," Sam said gently. "I was afraid you'd be hurt. Everyone else in town couldn't wait to jump to the conclusion that I opened that bookstore to take you for a ride. I had to hope that you knew me better than that. I'm not your ex-husband. I'd cut off an arm before using you, but I wasn't absolutely positive you realized that. You *do* trust me, Valentine."

"I'm mad enough to strangle you with my bare hands and you want to talk about trust?" She backed up another step. "You actually opened that store to sell *my* books? Didn't it once strike you that the whole idea was insane?"

"Actually, no. It struck me as an amazingly easy way to get you out of hock—at least temporarily. All I'm out is a couple of months' rent, which you can pay me back. The stock's all yours. I don't have to order, I don't have to know anything about the book busi-ness, and I've got volunteer help for most of the day. My hardest job is raking in the cash. If there's a teensy deception involved, no one is hurt by it. You stay sol-vent. Your customers are getting merchandise they want. Everybody's happy."

"Read my lips, Sam. I am *not* happy."

"Did you expect a good friend to stand by and watch you get hurt without doing a damn thing?"

He phrased the question calmly, reasonably, in a voice softer than velvet. He was trying to trick her, Val thought darkly. And doing a nerve-jangling good job of it. They were still moving. Until that instant she hadn't realized it, but she seemed to have backed up past the cookbooks, past the self-help section, unconsciously turned—into Civil War history—and the devil was still coming toward her.

Her pulse skittered nervously and her palms were suddenly slicker than slides. Nothing was going right. Sam just wasn't behaving as though he believed she was angry. Deliberately she raised her voice another octave. "You went behind my back!"

"Only because you wouldn't have let me help you anyway."

"That isn't the point! I didn't ask for your help. I didn't want it. I told you honestly how I felt—that I had problems, but they were problems I needed to solve on my own. You just ignored me—interfered in my life with no respect for my feelings—and I'd call that crossing an unforgivable line."

"Ah," Sam murmured thoughtfully. "So if the situation were reversed and I was the one in trouble up to my neck, you'd have politely turned your back? Done nothing? Like you've done nothing for Lincoln and Jonesey?"

Val scowled at him. "It's not the same thing! I don't want you involved!"

"And that's the bottom line, isn't it, honey? It would be dangerous for me to be involved with a bad, bad woman like you."

Sam clearly meant to tease her, but the comment struck Val like the jab of a needle. No, she'd never thought of herself as *bad* like some treasonous Mata Hari. But Sam was a good man with a lot of protective knight in his character. He didn't know about all the people she'd disappointed. He didn't know that she'd somehow managed to hurt anyone who ever loved her. "Shepherd. I want you to undo that bookstore. Forget the whole idea. Forget me. Go home."

He said quietly, "No more trying to be friends?"

She closed her eyes. She'd rather die than reject Sam, but it had to be better to make a clean break than risk hurting him worse later. "No."

"Good," he murmured. "Because I never once wanted to be friends with you, honey."

Her eyes shot open in confusion. Too late. Sam took one last step closer, trapped her neatly against the paneled wall between two bookshelves and angled his head.

Hindsight came seconds too late. She could have, should have, foreseen that Sam had a purpose in backing her into a corner. But in that first second, Val simply never anticipated a kiss. Her entire concentration had been focused on being tough and mean—her hands were even coiled into fists, in anticipation of socking him...in anticipation of *leveling* him, if that's what she had to do, to un-embroil Shepherd from her life.

But faster than she could think, slower than she could breathe, his warm lips were moving over hers. Gently. Wooingly. Intimately.

It was satin black in that corner. The illumination from his battery lantern only provided a distant glow. Her flashlight...she didn't know what she'd done with the flashlight. Val told herself, promised herself, that she'd have bludgeoned him with the flashlight if she'd just had it, because dammit, he'd tricked her again.

But that helpful blunt instrument was nowhere in sight or reach. Slowly Sam lifted her tight-clenched fists and laid them around his neck—as if he expected her to obediently keep them there—and then kissed her again, a dark kiss, a wild kiss, a kiss so dizzyingly deep that her heart stopped dead . . . and then fluttered like dove's wings.

Pelting, melting kisses trailed the line of her jaw to her throat. Her skin temperature climbed to a hundred and ten. Cool air feathered her abdomen when he pushed up her sweatshirt and in the same smooth motion unsnapped the hook of her bra. It was so dark. Her breath caught like a tangled thread when his palm cupped her breast.

"Sam—"

"Shh."

Somewhere, miles away, she heard rain battering against windows. She could smell leather bindings and books, feel the cool paneled wall against her back, and knew those things were real. But not nearly as real as Sam. Her hands were no longer tucked in fists, but pushing through his thick springy hair. She saw his eyes, liquid and dark, when he felt her nipple contract in his palm.

She was aroused. That wasn't news. Her knees were turning into sponges, and her heart was thumping wicked, erotic, disgracefully sentimental love songs. That wasn't news, either. She'd always gone crazy when Sam touched her, but that was only a measure of the shameless weakness in her character.

"Shepherd—"

"Shh."

His tongue stroked her right nipple. Slowly. Then her left nipple. Slowly. In a single motion he loosened the thin satin ribbon holding back her hair, and the mass tumbled over his hands. She felt herself sinking somewhere deep and soft. She'd felt that liquid sensation of falling with him before, but not like this. She was very sure. Not like this.

"Sam?" Her voice sounded thicker than clotted cream. Her plan to act tough and mean . . . she should have known it was hopeless. Her plan to just stay friends . . . she should have known that was hopeless, too. Her pulse hummed like the sing of a high wire. Weakness was invading her body like a silky immersion underwater, a weakness for him, a weakness too powerful for her to deny. If she was going to make another unforgivable mistake, though, she had to be sure that he wasn't hurt by it. "Sam, I don't want you to love me."

"Okay."

"I want you."

"I know, honey. I want you, too."

"But if you want to make love, it has to be . . . just sex. No calling it anything else."

"Okay."

His lips were buried in her throat. She had to tug on his ears to bring his face up to hers. "Don't say 'okay.' Every time you 'okay,' it means you want me to think you're agreeing with me. I want you to *mean* it, Sam. No deep waters. No commitments. No falling in love."

He heard her out. And then reached for the ribbed edge of her sweatshirt. "You can stop worrying, Red. There's no chance of my falling in love with you." He unraveled the fabric over her head, peeling off the loose straps of her bra with it, and dropped both garments behind him. "If you want to be honest, I'll be honest, too. All I ever cared about was getting you in bed. Sex. Unforgettably hot sex. That's all I want from you."

His tone was convincingly serious. Val caught her breath, aware that most women hoped to hear treasuring, tender words from a lover—but she wasn't most women. Sam couldn't be hurt if all he wanted was sex, and his blunt words enormously reassured her.

For all of three seconds.

When his long lean arms swept around her, something in his eyes made her shiver. He claimed her mouth in a cherishing kiss, a sharing of tastes and textures and promises, a kiss so soft that her knees started wobbling. He seemed to know that was a problem, because he gently drew her down. The scratchy carpet cushioned her spine, but lying with him, lying next to him proved no solution to her problem at all.

His hand buried in her thick cascades of hair, holding her still. He buffed her breasts with his lips and tongue and the nuzzling edge of his whiskered cheek, not roughly, not even arousingly, but as if he hadn't mentioned before that he found them flawless. Then slowly, as if he was afraid of scaring her, his fingertip rimmed the waistband of her jeans.

Every feminine nerve in her body promptly electrified. His thumb flicked the snap open. She heard the sound in the darkness, saw the look on his face. The zipper parted when his big hands slid inside, riding the sides of her bare hips as he chased the jeans down, inch by slow inch, his lips skimming every one of those inches until her jeans were lying in a puddle near her feet.

If there was oxygen anywhere in the atmosphere, Val would have clawed to claim it. Leisurely his mouth climbed back up, from her instep to her ankle, from ankle to calf to the inside of her thigh. And the whole time, the whole impossible time Sam was shamelessly sabotaging her ability to think or breathe, he was talking, talking, talking.

"I don't give a damn about you." His whisper was bourbon smooth, as soft and wicked as a lover's caress. "I can't imagine where you got the insane idea that I cared about anything more than your body."

"Don't—"

"A quick selfish lay. That was all I had in mind. A scratch of an itch. A roll in the sack. I can't believe you were crazy enough to worry that I actually felt something deep for you—"

"Shut up, Sam."

"You could beat me with a horsewhip, tar and feather, torture me. Nothing could make me love you. The moon would turn green before I could conceivably give a royal hoot about you, Valentine—"

She catapulted toward him. He was too damn big to shake, so she kissed him. Long and hard, with her arms wrapped inescapably around his stubborn neck, and her heart aching with helplessness. She wasn't fooled by all his silly words. The witless man gave more than a royal hoot. He loved her. His eyes exposed a soul-dark loneliness. His touch communicated naked fears and raw emotions, laying himself vulnerable the way no man did—and never Sam—unless he was sure of his lover. Sure she cared. Sure she wouldn't hurt him.

How was she supposed to protect a man who didn't have a brain in his head?

A loud roaring filled her ears, as though the tumultuous storm outside had sneaked in. Sam broke away from the hopeless, helpless assault of her kisses, but not for long. Mutely she watched him shuck off his sweatshirt, peel off his jeans. And then he came back to her, stunningly bare.

She had no time to warn him that she was going to be a disappointment, but he seemed to sense she was afraid. A mistake, she thought fleetingly. A disastrous mistake to let Sam know she was afraid of anything to do with him, because the result was just as cataclysmic as exposing pure oxygen to flame.

They came together in a sensual tangle, with Sam terribly out of control and unreasonably, deliberately, attacking any hope she had of keeping hers. Windows rattled in a gusty wind; sheets of rain drilled on the roof, and Val had never once thought of a bed of sweatshirts as being romantic. But it was. With him. Letting go...she'd never imagined being able to let go like this, never fathomed the power of being needed the way Sam needed her, never dreamed the wild sweet sense of rightness he made her feel.

He swore once. Grappling in the velvet shadows for the pocket of his jeans. But in seconds he'd taken care of protection and was back, her devil lover, with her vulnerability intimately on his mind. He made her ache with need. He made her hurt with longing. And when she was burning up, shuddering with emotions from the inside out, pepper hot, her skin coated with the same silky sheen as his, he took her on a long winsome ride through the stormy night...to a place where a woman could express every fear, every feeling and still know herself loved. Infinitely loved. Exquisitely loved.

It took a while before Sam's heartbeat simmered down. Afraid of crushing her, he shifted their positions so Val was sprawled on his chest. She didn't protest. Thankfully his redhead was too wasted to protest much of anything. Making him smile, she nuzzled her cheek in the curve of his shoulder and wriggled once, then nestled against the length of him with all the abandon of a tired puppy.

They needed to move soon. They could hardly spend the night in her store, cramped between book-shelves on bare carpet, yet Sam was in no hurry. He should have known that his hellion would eventually incite him into making love in an inappropriate time and place. He also should have known that a proper bed and a romantically set stage made no difference, not with Valentine. They hadn't just been good to-gether. They had been soul-shakingly unforgettable.

Val stirred. Alarmed, Sam carefully lulled her into catnapping a little longer by stroking her hair. Far too soon, his sleepy love was likely to waken and remem-ber that she'd been mad enough to strangle him.

Protectively, possessively, Sam sifted her hair through his fingers. Truthfully, she'd taken his "rival store" idea better than he expected. She didn't like his knowledge or interference in her money problems. But that aggravation seemed to distract her from noticing the obvious—there were far easier ways he could have sneaked her some financial help. A farfetched scheme like fronting a store was ridiculously unneces-sary... if he didn't have a second ulterior motive.

There were no guarantees that the store would suc-cessfully stir the town against him—and turn them all on Val's side—but he believed there was a chance. Their enemy had always been Ron, not Valentine. Sam had the opportunity to seem an identical scoundrel to Ron. And he'd heard all the stories being circulated and embellished and deliciously retold about Valentine's youth, but they were the stuff of gossip and entertainment, not real enmity. No one, ever, had hated Val. When Ron hurt them, they'd latched onto the handiest scapegoat and lost sight of who their real enemy was. Sam believed, hoped, his "store" would force them to reopen their eyes.

The irony of the situation hadn't escaped him. If his plan was successful, he'd be facing a lynch mob before long.

It was a far cry from the charging white knight of a hero he'd wanted to be for Val. But needs must where the devil drove, Sam thought. Winning his lady couldn't be accomplished by spiriting her off. Valentine accused him of never listening, but he'd always listened—and understood. She *did* have a problem she had to solve for herself. He couldn't tell her she was good and expect her to believe him, because faith in herself had to come from within. Valentine was used to being found wanting, used to thinking of herself as a disappointment. Until she started trusting herself and her feelings Sam didn't have a beggar's prayer of the kind of commitment he wanted from her.

He hoped, though, that making love had made a difference. She'd been scared. He knew. She'd responded on the impulse of the moment, and impulsiveness was a condemnable trait in Val's eyes. He knew that, too. And she was the one who had to change her mind about herself, but damned if she could conceivably, ever, imagine that *he* saw her as a disappointment after that.

She wriggled against him. He heard her soft sigh, a sensual, kittenish sound of laziness and contentment.

Sam held his breath. If her still waters didn't run so damn deep, he might almost be convinced that Val had figured out she was the most lovable woman on the circumference of the globe and felt smug-silly wonderful about it.

"Sam..." she whispered. "I never thought we'd fit."

"No?" There was a smile in her voice, a hint of teasing. What he'd hoped for, but definitely not what he'd been expecting.

"No. You're too tall. I'm too small. You can't even kiss me unless I'm on tiptoe, and even then you have to hunch over."

"Did you happen to notice that those problems handily disappear when we're lying down?"

"We can't be prone every time we kiss."

"We could try," Sam murmured, and won a chuckle from her. A soft, natural chuckle.

Warily he angled his head to sneak a peek at her face. Val chose the same moment to cross her arms on her personal mattress, his chest, and prop her chin in a palm. Her skin, Sam noted, was flushed the shade of a moonlit pearl, her mouth blush red from his kisses. The sparkle of sass in her eyes would seem to indicate that she felt confident and comfortable with him and the new intimacy between them. She looked...well loved. She looked...loving and incomparably beautiful and as if she had no memory of ever fighting with him.

Sam's pulse started skittering nervously. He traced the edge of her lips with his fingertips. "You're wearing a pretty silly smile, Red," he whispered.

"Maybe you're a pretty good lover."

"What is this 'maybe'?"

"It'll just go to your head if I confess you were superb enough to shake my timbers, Shepherd."

"If you wiggle your timbers any more provocatively, I'm probably going to get the idea that you like driving me out of my mind."

Her eyes met his. "Did I? Drive you out of your mind?"

There, he thought. A trace of that terrible vulnerability she worked so hard to hide. "You did worse than that. Here I'd hoped to overwhelm you with my incredible prowess as a lover, and instead you made me forget everything I ever knew. I didn't just *want* you, Valentine. It was more than possible that I would have died if I couldn't have you. Think what it would have been like living with that on your conscience for the rest of your life . . . there's that smile again."

"What smile?"

"That smug, feminine smile. I like it." Sam more than liked it. He was afraid to breathe for fear of doing anything to upset that fragile glow in her eyes, the easiness and sense of rightness between them. On the other hand, he couldn't take much more stress without causing himself a heart attack. He murmured, "I think I'm going to shoot myself for asking this, but how come I'm not hearing second thoughts and a worried commentary on how this can never happen again?"

"Would it do any good to tell you that we'll never make love again?"

"No."

"This whole evening started out," she mentioned, "with my firm and determined intention to kick you out of my life. Even if I had to level you to accomplish it."

"You did level me," he assured her.

She stroked his cheek, but her smile was fleeting. "When I first met you, I thought you were one of the rarest of endangered species—a nice guy. But I was wrong. You fight dirty and you don't play fair. When you think something is right, you just do it, no matter what anyone else says or thinks. You've been trying to take a bullet for me from the minute you flew into town. I've tried everything short of renting a bulldozer to stop you. Nothing works."

"I could change," Sam suggested.

"You're not going to change."

"I could try."

"You could try," Val agreed, "but I'm afraid that hero mentality runs awfully deep in your character. It'd be easier for me to do the changing. Which is what I've decided to do. I certainly haven't made any headway playing by my rules, so from now on we're going to play the game entirely by yours."

"I'm not sure what all that means," Sam said cautiously.

"It means that the two of us aren't going to work," she murmured. "I love you, Shepherd. I love you like an ache in my heart, and you're too smart not to realize that I'd never have made love with you if I didn't. So...you win. You have a lover if you want one. And I fully intend to enjoy loving you. Until you've had enough."

For months, he'd dreamed of hearing words of love from her. But not quite like this. His stomach was churning enough acid to start an ulcer. "Enough?"

"You'll eventually see," she said gently, "that I'm not the right woman for you. But I realize now that I can't force you to see that. I can't protect you from making a mistake. All I can do is be completely honest with you. You're not really in love with me, Sam."

"You sound very sure."

She nodded seriously. "I don't think the thought would have even crossed your mind if I hadn't been fighting you. I can't imagine many women would ever fight you. You're just not used to it, and you love a challenge. The whole pursuit and chase is fun. But I'm not going to be any kind of a challenge anymore. Before long I'm positive that you'll understand that...Sam?...*Sam!*"

He understood, as he rolled her beneath him, that Valentine was drawing her battle lines.

She didn't stop him from chaining a row of kisses down her long white neck, but he both saw, and felt, the pulse in her throat start to gallop. He thought longingly of the big, soft, comfortable double bed in her house and could scarcely believe she'd driven him—and twice in the same night—into making love in her damned store.

But apparently he'd failed to make it clear the first time. She was not the wrong woman for him, but the perfect one. The only woman where the whole world came right when they were together. And before Valentine built up any more insane illusions that he'd soon "get enough of her"...he hated to argue with a woman, but that was definitely a misconception that he needed to correct. Now. Promptly and thoroughly. Even if it took him all night.

Heaven knows how Val could possibly believe that she presented no challenge to him.

The redhead had his heart in a wringer. Maybe sixty years from now, he'd see the humor. She was stubbornly determined to protect him from the only thing he wanted.

Her.

Eight

Val awakened several minutes before the alarm. For the third morning this week it was raining. Gray diamonds drizzled down the windowpanes and the house was gloomier than a tomb.

She didn't want to get up. She wanted to wrap herself around a warm male body and snuggle. Maybe more than snuggle. Her mind envisioned a sleeping Sam, waking slowly to her provocative kisses until he was wildly turned on, drugged with desire, completely at her mercy. She would make love to him exactly—*exactly* as he'd made love to her. She'd tempt, taunt, tease. She'd take everything he'd taught her about earthy sensuality and use it, with dazzling feminine ruthlessness, against him. She'd make him so hot he thought he was dying. She'd ...

Irritably Val swung her legs over the side of the bed. There was no body beside her to tempt, taunt and tease. And no earthly reason why her mind *persisted* in plaguing her with such disgraceful, foolish fantasies when she was sleeping alone. It had been six days since she'd thrown away all pride and volunteered to be Sam's lover, offering terms that most men would jump for—no strings, no worries, no need for trumped-up promises.

Sam hadn't made a pass since. They'd spent every evening together. The electricity between them was hot enough to scorch rock, so Val could hardly assume that he'd come to his senses and lost interest.

If they weren't making love, it was because Shepherd, damn him, didn't like her terms.

A chilly dampness had invaded the whole house. Val shivered as she yanked off her white silk nightgown. Bleary-eyed, she laid out pearls and a navy blue suit from her closet and then stumbled toward the bathroom. Work, she thought. She needed to think about work instead of Sam, Sam, Sam.

She flipped on the bathroom light switch, reached for her toothbrush... and abruptly sniffed. Pivoting around, she saw the contents of her bathtub. Hyacinths. The tub was literally chock-full of pots of hyacinths, whites and lavenders, their heady sweet scent an irresistible anecdote to a dark gloomy day.

When she walked into the living room, she found daisies. Everywhere. In every dark corner, every niche, every spare surface. Vases full of silly, fragile, frivolous, cheerful daisies. All yellow. Her favorite color, yellow.

In the kitchen, it was pansies. Bowls of floppy pansies covered her whole counter space with their silky-soft petals and vibrant colors.

There was no card, no sign of the donor, and Val told herself that there was no way, absolutely none, that Sam could have gotten them into the house. He'd driven her home last night promptly at eleven and kissed her at the door. Actually, he'd laid her against the door and kissed her witless, kissed her senseless, kissed her until there was no question in her mind that they'd end up in bed *that* night . . . but then he'd left. And Val had nothing better to do while she'd been pacing the floor in frustration than be sure her doors were locked.

He couldn't have gotten in. But he had.

There was no avoiding the sight or scent of those flowers. Not when she dressed, not when she popped a slice of bread in the toaster for breakfast, not when she fixed her hair in a forties-style chignon. By the time she climbed into the car to head for work, her heart was humming old, corny, sickly sentimental love songs. This, while trying to drive in a wild banshee rain on a black doom-gloom morning with thunder and lightning all around her. *You think I care, Shepherd? You think you're getting to me? You think I'm gonna do something stark-raving foolish just because I think you're wonderful?*

She whipped into her customary parking spot in the alley, snapped off the windshield wipers and defroster, and then made a mad race through the puddles for the door. It was only eight-thirty. The store should have been dead quiet, yet she heard voices the moment she ducked inside. Men's voices, sounding low and excited. Peeling off her raincoat, she aimed for the pool of light spilling into the hall from her office.

One look, and a lump swelled in her throat. A big, thick, unswallowable lump. Quite obviously, Sam hadn't slept at all last night. And there were two places, not one, that he'd broken into.

In a space too cramped for mice, both the sheriff and Jonesey had found enough space to make themselves at home—Harold on her desk, and Jonesey in her office chair. Both of them were chortling like schoolboys. The sheriff was rolling quarters. Jonesey was wetting his thumb and counting greenbacks. Except for Harold's considerable behind, her desk was literally a sea of money. Copper, silver, and a shovelful of loose green bills.

Neither man noticed she was there until Val cleared her throat. "I don't suppose it occurred to either of you that in some rare, obscure segments of society, a person's private finances are actually considered nobody else's business?"

"Now, sweetheart. When I noticed the light on and realized Jonesey was in here early, I naturally stopped by to say hello. It was accidental I stayed to help him. He was trying to get this all ready before the bank opened. Don't get your liver in an uproar. In fact, pour yourself a mug and relax," Harold said genially, and then to Jonesey, "I can't *believe* the haul he sneaked in here last night."

"Electric bill. Rent. Insurance—hell, I thought she was gonna lose it...." Jonesey could hardly work his stogie around a rusty-sounding guffaw. "You should have told me from the start what he was up to, Val. Not that I didn't realize what was happening to the inventory right quick. But for a short while there, I thought he was a low-down skulking traitor trying to run you out of business."

Val hadn't moved. "He agreed with me. That he wasn't going to do this anymore. We sat down and talked about it days ago. I told him I didn't want money that came from fooling people, it wasn't ethical, it wasn't right. He said okay, that he'd just sell off the inventory he started with and that would be that."

Neither man seemed interested in this announcement. She tried again. "To be absolutely sure we were on the same wave length, I made him open his wallet. The copy of my store key he'd made—I took it back. Which would have made it very, very difficult for him to get in the store at night. Unless he had help."

Both men were as silent as deaf mutes.

"Jonesey? Did you give him a key?"

Jonesey couldn't look at her because he was suddenly so busy talking to Harold. "Quit playing with the change, Sheriff. I need help banding the bills. The bank's going to be open in another twenty minutes."

"Okay, okay. It's just that I love the feel of the coins. Reminds me of the time I took Martha to Vegas and she won at the slots. Filled two buckets..."

It was useless trying to talk to either one of them. After hanging her raincoat on the hook in the bathroom, she wound her way to the front of the store. She unlocked the front door, switched the Closed sign to Open, and then simply leaned in the alcove of the display window.

Lightning streaked the sky. Tires sprayed a hiss of water every time a car passed. Few pedestrians were braving the weather unless they had to. And across the street, five doors down, lights flipped in Sam's store.

He'd worked yesterday, taken her out that evening, spent the wee hours of the morning with his time divided between delivering flowers and playing highwayman, and now was back at work again. It added up, Val thought, to a man who had absolutely no sleep.

Because of her.

In the background she heard the sound of the men's laughter and low-pitched chatter. Jonesey had very quickly figured out what was happening to "his" inventory. The sheriff hadn't added two and two until the second night, when he caught Sam carrying boxes of books down the street in broad moonlight.

Probably she should have expected that her friends would join Robin Hood's band without a qualm. There was money in her till. Money to finally pay bills. She'd been nearly bankrupt, and they hadn't found a way to help her. Sam had. They all thought—even little Lincoln—that Shepherd was the cleverest man ever born and a hero to boot.

Val stared at the lights in his store window, aware of all he'd done with her and feeling her heart pound with anxiety. She loved that man. But all the crazy feelings he'd had only intensified her fears that it was wrong, very wrong, to let the relationship continue.

If Sam had just settled for an affair, she wouldn't feel so scared. Instead, as soon as she'd offered those terms, Sam had shut her down as fast as a scold. By courting her knight-and-lady style, he didn't need to shout his intentions in her ear. She got the message. Sam wanted rings. Commitment. Tangling vows. All or nothing.

But her love was an idealist, and Val saw herself as grounded in reality. A hero needed a heroine. A good man, of honor and courage, needed a woman who matched him in goodness and honor and courage. For any two people to make it, they had to meet each other as equals. She would only disappoint Sam if she couldn't stand on her own.

And she was hardly doing that. Val squeezed her eyes closed. She'd come home to Chekapee, so sure that she was strong enough to turn her life around. But she'd tried everything she knew. Perseverance. Turning the other cheek. Being careful and helpful, never asking for thanks, and being as good a woman as she knew how to be. Nothing she'd done had mattered a whit. The people she grew up with were always going to associate her with Ron, with her jinx-prone mistakes of the past.

Coming home had been another mistake in judgment, she thought. But this failure stung. It stung like a wasp bite, stung deep at the level of belief in herself. And how could she possibly take the risk of commitment to Sam, when her scorecard of success in relationships didn't have a single win?

Shepherd, you just can't keep staying up nights for me. I've already caused you endless complications and trouble, and I can't—won't—risk disappointing you. Not you. Dammit, Sam, I'd never put back the pieces if I somehow managed to hurt you.

Val turned away from the window, thinking hard. Thanksgiving was only days away. Her parents had asked her down for the holiday, but Sam was here, and originally the last—absolutely last—thing she wanted to do was expose him to that kind of family gathering. She knew how it would go.

She knew, humiliatingly well, *exactly* how it would go.

But she'd live through it, she told herself firmly. It was an ideal opportunity to force Sam to take off any rose-colored glasses he had about her. And a woman who loved, who really loved, somehow found the courage to do what she had to do.

Sam's eyes were bloodshot and he had a tension headache the size of Texas. His energy tank was on empty. He wasn't sure how many straight hours he'd been up, but it was somewhere past thirty. He could probably fall asleep in a straight chair, and his smile felt pasted on.

He squinted at his watch. It was just past four. Ample time for him to hit the motel, shower and catch a snooze before picking up Valentine and Linc for dinner at seven. The volunteer manning the cash register could easily cope alone. Unfortunately if he left now, he'd miss the chance to communicate directly with his customers.

And there were at least two still in the store that he couldn't afford to miss.

He aimed first for Miss Holmes. The English teacher had been in every day after school, dressed invariably in polyester, with her spectacles hanging from a black rope around her neck. She always bought books, and always hid her sci-fi paperbacks under a concealing cover of classics. Her hunger for books, Sam could appreciate, but the old bat *really* came in to dish the dirt. The instant she spotted him, Sam could have sworn that her pointy little ears wriggled with pleasure. "I never imagined, Mr. Shepherd, how justified I feel that you've opened this store. I now have a way to indulge my reading habit without having to do business with *her.*"

"A lot of people in town tell me that." Deliberately Sam forced a confiding tone. "I hear Ms. Shroeder isn't going to be in business long."

"No?"

Sam shrugged. "The last I heard, her phone was going to be cut off if she couldn't pay the back bill. It sounded to me as if she were pretty near the end of her rope."

Miss Holmes's ample bosom swelled with righteous satisfaction, but then those healthy lungs seemed to deflate. She hesitated. "Valerie isn't *really* near the end of her rope, of course. Her parents have plenty of money."

"I wouldn't know about that. All I heard was that she took on that store completely on her own. Put every last cent she could borrow into it. But who cares? It's what you all want, to see her go under, isn't it?"

Miss Holmes opened her mouth to respond, and instead fell silent. She stared at him, suddenly looking disconcerted. *Good,* Sam thought. *Let that sink good and deep on your conscience, Petunia.*

"Excuse me, Miss Holmes."

He headed next for the pair of gossipers near the cash register. Sue Ellen, the broad-faced, broad-beamed woman who managed a gas station, was apparently an old school chum of Rose Wilkins. Sue Ellen inhaled any tome on engines and mechanics, no matter how thick. The realtor generally stopped in sometime during the afternoon to see how her rental investment was thriving.

"Well, hi, darlin'." Before he had the chance to return the greeting, Rose put a cloyingly affectionate hand on his biceps. "We were just talking about you. You've really done it! I've never seen a store be such an instant success." She added wickedly, "I went by Valerie's and she didn't have a customer in the place."

"Made you feel good, did it?"

Rose stroked his arm. "I think it's making everybody feel good. Revenge is sweet, you know? And hell, honey, if a woman can't stand a little heat, she'd better get out of the fire."

"I'm really glad you feel that way." Sam rolled his shoulders as if to chase out the day's kinks, a motion that effectively dislodged her passion-pink fingernails from his arm. "Some people might see it as mean, a stranger coming into town, taking one of their own down. Where I come from, it takes a wolf with a cutthroat instinct to make it in business. It's not my fault she's such easy prey. All's fair in the jungle, right, Rose?"

The tiniest frown appeared on Rose's forehead. "I . . . right."

"And all of you have helped me so much. You've made it so easy." Sam smiled at Sue Ellen. "I mean, none of you would care no matter what happens to her, right?"

Sue Ellen started to say something, then abruptly closed her mouth.

So did Sam. It was exhausting work, forcing people to rethink what they'd been doing to his Valentine. He knew he was making headway. More than a few of the good townspeople were nervously getting the idea that they'd invited a viper like Ron in their midst. But for now, he had to quit. The subtleties of viper role-playing simply took more concentration than he had. His vision was blurring, he was so stumbling tired.

He needed a shower. He needed some sleep. Though he didn't want to admit it, discouragement was starting to take him down. The store project was both keeping Val in money and giving him the means to make people relook at how they'd treated Valentine. It was working, but ultimately the effect was no more than a Band-aid on a surface set of sores. Val had other, deeper hurts. Hurts he couldn't fix. Love helped healing. Sam believed that. But whether he could coax his redhead to reach out for him, for love, for everything he believed they could have together... dammit, he didn't know.

It preyed on his mind, like a toothache he couldn't ignore, that all too possibly it wasn't fear or hurts holding her back but a far nastier problem. Maybe she really didn't love him. Not as he loved her. Maybe nothing he did or said could make her care. Not as he cared.

A half hour later, Sam was back in his motel room and listening to his chief support of support on the telephone. When the whole world was giving him hell, Sam could always count on his brother for backup and a buck up.

"Snake," Cole told him bluntly, "I think you've lost your mind. What the hell is this women doing to you? And I don't want to answer that. I want you to listen to me."

The telephone call had interrupted Sam midshower. He'd answered it soaking wet, but had ample time to dry off and sling the white towel around his neck while they covered air-freight business. Now, carrying the phone, he sank stark naked into the oversize chair by the window and half closed his eyes.

From the moment Cole used the nickname "Snake," Sam knew he wasn't going to get a backup and a buck up, but a lecture from an older brother who occasionally went into protective overdrive. And Sam valued his brother's opinion. But the punch line of this particular conversation was probably going to be the same whip he'd been beating himself up with all day. "Okay, okay, I'm listening."

"You got all A's in school. Ran rings around me. Maybe you went off the deep end for a while after Mom and Dad died, but that was the only time I ever saw you lose it. You pulled yourself out of that, got your pilot's license, set your course on an air-freight business, just kept plowing through any problems that came your way. You could have screwed up in a hundred ways, but you never lost that level head. Now you've paid off the bank and you're rolling it in really good, and I can't think of a time there wasn't a woman in your life. But you were always smart about the women you picked, too. They always had personality, a head on their shoulders, good legs, good sense..."

Sam slumped deeper in the chair. A groggy yawn escaped him. He already knew his own biography. Unless his brother had something else to say, Sam was afraid he was falling asleep. "Cole? Do you and Regan need to get back to Cripple Creek?"

"Hell, no. We can stay here until spring. In fact, that's how Regan wants to work it—a couple months in Chicago every winter. Would you stick to the subject?" Cole's voice climbed with frustration. "You've been down there nearly a month. How much time can it take for two people to figure out if they have something going? Every time I talk to you, you sound more torn up. You *never* went off the deep end over a woman before. Now this is nuts, Snake. There are other fish in the sea. Some things aren't meant to work out. Then you gotta call it quits and let it go. Come on home. Forget her. Sam? Dammit, Sam, are you there?''

Sam never meant to drop the phone, but through a gap in the curtains he saw a slight figure in the parking lot, standing under the Lazy Day Motel sign. A woman. A woman with russet-red hair and a strawberry-soft mouth, who was twisting her purse straps between her fingers and craning her head to read the numbers on the motel room doors.

Nothing miraculously changed in that instant. He was still reeling exhausted. The doubts plaguing him all day didn't suddenly disappear. And his brother had accurately perceived that he was in trouble.

But all Sam had to do was look at her to feel a familiar sinking sensation low in his gut. Nobody else had ever given him that feeling. It came with her. Only with her.

She'd spotted his room number but still stood there a minute, gnawing on her lip. And then she straightened her shoulders, squared her jaw and started crossing the parking lot. Toward his door.

"Snake? For cripes' sakes, where'd you go?"

Sam grabbed the phone. "Everything's fine. Talk to you later. Give Regan a kiss."

"*Sam—*"

He hung up the receiver, jerked the towel from his neck and whipped it around his waist, then banged his shin on the chair leg on the way to the door. He opened it so quickly that Val came close to knocking on his chest. She blinked in surprise. Why ever she'd come, she seemed to have completely forgotten how important a respectable reputation was to her. He hauled her inside before anyone could see her in a motel room doorway with a half-naked man, a half-naked man whose towel was slipping. He grabbed for it.

"Oh, God. I must have interrupted your shower. I knew I should have called first. And you probably think it's nuts, my coming here, when we were going to meet in just a couple hours for dinner. But Linc was going to be there then, and I wanted to talk to you alone first. For one thing, I wanted to ask you if you might want to have dinner with my parents on Thanksgiving—"

"It's okay, honey." The towel fought him. Viciously. It didn't want to knot and it didn't want to stay put, and he couldn't keep his eyes off her face. He'd sworn off making love with her until she realized he was playing for keeps. But at that exact moment, he had to admit his willpower wasn't terribly strong. Raindrops glistened in her hair. Her mouth looked soft and vulnerable, her skin infinitely touchable. She didn't need to make a dozen nervous excuses why she was here. She was here. To see him. All that could possibly matter. "Did you like the flowers?"

"Oh, Sam..."

The expression in her eyes immediately softened, giving him a heady, masculine feeling of satisfaction. All day he'd thought about her waking up to the surprise of a houseful of flowers. His self-doubting redhead needed more than some paltry little nosegay. Truthfully she needed a lot more than flowers to plump up her confidence. But she liked them. He could see in her face that she really liked them. He smiled at her happily.

"The flowers were beyond wonderful. Unbelievably beautiful. You're crazy to do something so special for me. I . . . good grief." Her tone abruptly changed. "Lord, Shepherd, you're so dead on your feet that you're weaving—"

"Me? I'm fine." It was the way she pushed the damp hair away from his brow. Possessively. As if she owned the right to touch him. It made something inside him ease, as if right now, at least, he just didn't have to worry about anything more. Though he never meant to let it happen, his eyelids shuttered to half-mast, then closed. He tried to open them again and did. But it was hard. They felt heavier than lead.

Vaguely he heard her purse being tossed somewhere. Vaguely he was aware that he'd lost the war with the towel. Mostly he noticed that she couldn't keep her hands off him. Hell, he felt the same way about her.

"Forget dinner tonight. You're not going anywhere. And we'll talk about Thanksgiving another time. You big lug, how could you let yourself get in this shape because of me? And tarnation, Shepherd, don't you fall before I've got you in bed!"

Bossy, he thought. He'd always known that once Val gained real confidence, she'd be bossy and demanding in bed. When she lunged for him, he couldn't have been happier. He decided he'd give in just this once. But he'd better tell her where the protection was, because it sure wasn't on his mind.

"I'm gonna shoot you when you wake up. Strangle you with my bare hands. Take all two hundred pounds of you right over my knee—"

He heard her soft voice crooning to him. Then felt the cool smooth sheets floating over his skin. Val had

a belt on. He felt it digging into his hip for a second.
For reasons he couldn't fathom she still had all her
clothes on, but she was there. All that mattered. He
opened his eyes one last time to be sure, but her head
was right on the pillow, her body pinned seductively
beneath his.

She was hot for him. No question about it. And he
was gonna make it so good for her...

So good...

So...

Nine

It was a long drive from Chekapee to Ormond Beach, where her parents' condominium was located. In Chicago, on Thanksgiving, there'd likely be snow on the ground and wind roaring off the lake. Here the temperature was a mild sixty, the sun relentlessly bright, and the exotic scent of citrus pervaded the air. On the first part of the drive, they passed miles of groves. The oranges weren't orange at all, but yellowish, looking like heavy balls tucked in nests of dark, shiny green leaves. The variety was probably Valencias, Val told him, and for a while kept up a running commentary on the history of citrus in Florida.

Sam's mind wasn't on oranges.

Falling asleep on a woman, he thought morosely, was a major tactical mistake. Three days ago, when he'd wakened still groggy from a twenty-four-hour nap, Val had been there. She'd served him coffee and a take-out breakfast and a lecture. He'd been stark naked in bed; she'd been dressed like a schoolmarm and her voice had been sexy soft and throaty and as implacable as an armored tank.

It was done. His store project. She'd had enough. He was killing himself for her, and she was calling a halt to it. If she found any more money sneaked into her till, she was giving it to charity. If that didn't stop him, she'd burn it.

"I understand that you want to financially help me, Sam. But it isn't money I'm trying to win." She'd paced around his motel room, determined to make him understand. "I don't care about the store. I never did. I care about *them,* the people I grew up with. I care that they think I was part of my ex-husband's embezzlement scheme—that I would ever have done anything so terrible to people who were friends to me."

She'd slammed her hands into the big pockets of her skirt. "They think I'm a traitor. And I knew, coming home, that it wasn't going to be easy to change their minds. But I haven't done so many things right in my life, and this *mattered.* If I'd run away, I'd never have been able to come back. They would always have thought the worst of me. So I came home, and I've been an active part of the community. I've been here for my friends and family. I've shown them, every way I know how, that I care and have always cared. And if I can't win that way...by doing the right thing...then I don't want to win at all."

"Good's gonna win out in the end?"

She turned her head. "You think that's naive?"

"I think the cause of good needs a helping hand from time to time. Or a good kick in the seat of the pants. If you want me to close down that shindig of a store, I will. But I want another week, Valentine.''

''No.''

''One week. Seven short days. It's hardly a big deal—''

''No.''

He'd lurched out of bed and kissed her, this woman who never gave an inch, had too damn much pride, and would probably go to the wall for a principle. He was mad at her. For being like him. For not letting him help her when she needed help. Only somehow none of that frustrated anger seeped into the kiss. She willingly yielded in his arms, and suddenly there was nothing but her and a whoosh of sensations and textures, her scent, her taste, her melting up on tiptoe to lie against him, the feel of her fingertips on his cheek.

When she'd broken off the kiss, she'd been trembly, breathless. ''Okay,'' she'd whispered, ''you can have your week.''

Too late, Sam realized that her desperately sweet responsiveness had been motivated by guilt. Valentine hadn't given out a concession. She'd been gently closing a door. Once he packed in the store, he'd lose his excuse for staying in Chekapee. He'd have to go home. Away from her terrible influence. That damn guilt thing of hers! She saw herself as responsible for his being exhausted, for ''neglecting'' his business, for wasting his time on a woman who couldn't see her own self-worth with trifocals and a magnifying glass.

A week? How the hell was he gonna turn that around in a week? Sam felt as though the sands were shifting down the hourglass while he waited for the clunk of the guillotine. Panic was becoming as familiar as his own heartbeat. Half the days in that impossibly short week were already gone.

He was going to lose her. Unless something drastic happened soon.

Worse yet, he couldn't shake the restless, edgy feeling that there was something about this Thanksgiving dinner with her parents that he needed to know. Critically needed to know. And didn't.

"Turn here, Sam."

He turned. The smell of verdant ripening citrus had long changed to the tang of salt air. He'd come to love "her" ocean, but their treks to the shore had been limited to some of the wild, deserted beaches up the northern coast. It wasn't like that here. This strip was salted with pristine, pricey condominiums, packed so close that catching a view of the water was rare.

He tugged at the collar of his shirt. "Are you nervous about seeing your parents?"

"Nervous? Heavens, no. I haven't seen them in more than a month. I'm looking forward to it."

And she didn't, Sam thought, act nervous. But Val had been oddly persistent about including him in this Thanksgiving gathering. With any other woman, Sam would have leaped to the hopeful conclusion that she wanted her parents to meet a man she was seeing seriously. No dice. Valentine, far too carefully, had reassured him that extra guests were status quo at the Shroeders. She wouldn't have asked him if she thought he would be uncomfortable.

He was already uncomfortable. Something was going on here, but damned if he could figure out what it was.

Val flashed him a smile. "I promise, you'll have a good time. They're easy people to be around, Sam.

You'll like them. Everyone does. They love to entertain and they love company. Honestly, you'll enjoy
it."

Sam bought that like a sales pitch for ocean front-
age in Wyoming. The more assuring and reassuring
Val tried to be, the more he sensed a tricky Armaged-
don ahead. A battle. A test. With potentially drastic
stakes if he didn't do well.

At the last turn, Val burrowed in her purse for a
lipstick. If he wasn't so tense, he'd have smiled at the
feminine whim. Her lips didn't need the touch-up. She
didn't need anything. Sam had seen her dressed like a
goody-two-shoes. He'd seen her look like an undone
hellion racing down the beach. But he'd never seen her
look so classically elegant. Her makeup was flawless,
and her hair pinned back with ivory combs that
matched her ivory sheath. The dress draped her figure like an alluring shadow. Bone heels. Silk stockings that whispered seductively when she crossed her
legs. A scarf with gold threads tied just so around her
neck.

She was dressed to perfection.

And impossibly wrong.

The couple who answered the door were wearing
Hawaiian print shirts and casual slacks. Sam watched
Val take one glance at their clothes and gulp as though
she'd swallowed a frog.

Kisses and hugs were exchanged at the door, excla-
mations about how long since they'd seen each other.
Both parents were clearly delighted to see her, and Val
was smiling then. Smiling hard, as she whipped the
fancy scarf off her neck and pushed her formal high
heels unobtrusively under a chair.

Sam made an instinctive move toward her. It was blocked by an extended hand reaching out to pump his.

"Sam, is it? We're glad you could come. Miriam always makes enough food for an army. I'd be stuck eating turkey next July if we didn't have some help. We've got the Lions on in the den. The girls have orders not to let that bird get done until halftime."

Randolph Shroeder was a slim, slight man with thinning white hair and his daughter's hazel eyes. He was comfortable playing host and it showed. His smile was welcoming, his handshake warm and natural. Sam was handed a tall iced tea and eased into the gathering as if he'd never been a stranger. Which was very nice, except that he lost sight of Val.

"Sam, is it? Now it's Miriam, none of that Mrs. Shroeder nonsense. We gave up that kind of formality when we moved to the beach. Kick off your shoes. Heaven knows everyone else has. And let me introduce you around...."

Miriam was in her sixties, still pretty, with a regal posture and fading russet hair that softly framed her face. She handed him a plate of hors d'oeuvres, then ordered him not to eat them. She'd shoot him if he didn't have an appetite at dinner. Her smile was teasing, and her warm blue eyes reflected a Southern woman's traditional skill for making a man feel at ease.

Sam had never been inclined to like her parents. These were the people, after all, who'd first ingrained in Valentine that she was a disappointment. But as Val had claimed—as he'd never believed—they really were easy people to be around. For him.

Not for her.

An hour passed before Sam understood that there had never been a test *he* was supposed to pass. It was his redhead facing tests and Armageddons. And it was pretty damned obvious she'd faced them before.

Typical of some family gatherings, the men separated from the women. There were other guests, a fairly eclectic group. A neighbor with nowhere to go on the holiday, a lawyer friend, someone's brother-in-law, and a pair of distant Shroeder cousins. Sam was installed in an armchair in front of the Lions game with the rest of the men. If he craned his neck just so, he had a clear view of the dining table in the other room.

Never mind Miriam's claim to informality, the dining table was set to impress royalty. Which Miriam's daughter knew well. Sam watched Val go back and forth from the kitchen like an Olympic runner in a relay team. She filled Waterford crystal glasses with ice water, then carried in cranberry sauce, then butter molds formally carved to look like pineapples, then individual plates of artistically arranged salad.

She fussed like a worried hen. Wisps of hair started to curl around her cheeks. Then whole curling strands escaped the ivory combs. The other women in the kitchen were laughing. When her mother called her, she tensed. Then flew.

The whole damn table was perfect, but a basket of rolls slipped out of her hands. Right when her mother was standing in the doorway. Miriam laughed and said something consoling.

Randolph carved the turkey, making a jovial production out of it. Midmeal, a pea bounced off Valentine's fork and catapulted into someone's salad. It was the stuff of natural humor, not tragedy, and everyone laughed. Including Val. But Sam saw, with killing clarity, how all the color washed out of her face.

After dessert the women descended on the kitchen with Val in the lead. Miriam was kicked out and ordered to relax and enjoy her guests. She'd done all the cooking. But Sam noticed that the other women slowly drifted away from the kitchen, leaving Val alone with a mound of dishes that had to rival the Egyptian pyramids.

When he rose to help her, he found himself trapped. Miriam wanted to show him the condominium and balcony view, and she just kept talking. By then, Sam felt more tense than a too-taut rubber band, afraid to say anything for fear he'd snap. No one, even once, had asked Val about the bookstore or how she was doing in Chekapee. And he'd seen the condo. The place was light, airy and tastefully decorated, but nothing in it looked a year old. There were no knick-knacks, no old mementos, as if the Shroeders acknowledged no memories of their lives before moving to the beach. Put it all together, and Sam had the picture of Val growing up in a family where problems were ignored, mistakes not allowed, and any potentially uncomfortable subject swept swiftly under the rug. They loved their daughter. But they sure as hell had never let her talk.

A plate crashed in the kitchen. Miriam, motioning to their balcony view of the ocean, didn't even look up. "It's restful, we discovered. Living on the ocean. It's always so peaceful."

Randolph tried to talk him into an after-dinner drink. When Val finally appeared in the doorway, her dad affectionately put his arm around her. She looked pale. Worn. So fragile that a cross word would tear her down. She made a soap smudge on her ivory sheath and her hair was coming down. "I'm sorry, you two, but we really need to get going. I have to work in the morning," she said.

There was a fuss about them leaving too soon. The Shroeders clearly wanted their daughter to stay; they claimed they hadn't enough time with her and didn't see her often enough.

Sam couldn't wait to get her out of there.

When Sam handed her into the car, Val gratefully folded into the seat as if she were sinking into a marshmallow. She'd been on her feet for almost four hours straight. Sam's eyes were hooded against the glare of early evening sun when he crossed around the front of the car. She couldn't read his expression, and he said nothing when he climbed in and started the engine.

"Still full from dinner?" she asked him.

"Yes."

"I told you it would go fine, didn't I?"

"Yes, you did."

"They're good people, Sam. I knew you'd like them. When I was growing up, they entertained everyone from senators to any neighbor who stopped by the house. They both have a special sensitivity for making people feel at home and comfortable—"

A strange, rough sound came out of his throat. Her hand was halfway to pulling on the seat belt when he swiveled around, cocked up her chin and laid a bruising-hard kiss on her mouth. When he lifted his head, he said sharply, "Don't take this wrong, but I don't think I can hold a conversation about how 'sensitive' your parents are, or anything else about that dinner. I just don't want to talk right now. Okay?''

She nodded on a quick, rattled breath. Sam...she'd never heard him sound angry before. She'd also never seen his face set in such harsh, unyielding lines.

When she fumbled with the seat belt, he grabbed it and clinched the parts together for her. Moments later they were streaking down the highway. She still hadn't managed to swallow for the heartbeat stuck in her throat. His reaction, she told herself, shouldn't have surprised her. She'd asked for it, in fact, invited it. The whole purpose of taking Sam to meet her parents had been to force him to see her in a clearer, more realistic light.

Recalling the dreadful afternoon made her feel a familiar aching weariness. It was always the same. She tried. She always tried. In a hundred ways she'd always tried to be the daughter they wanted, and somehow ended up being a plate-breaking, pea-spilling klutz who couldn't even manage to dress right. Val couldn't think of a single time that she hadn't embarrassed her parents in company. Not at seven. And not at twenty-eight.

Spilling a pea wasn't a criminal offense. But take enough spilled peas and eventually the total picture was obvious. The people she grew up with knew her infinitely better than Sam. When it came to personal relationships, she was a screwup.

Miles swept past before she sneaked a peek at Sam's face. Dusky shadows filled the car as the sun went down. In the dim light, his profile looked forbidding and uncompromising, and her mind hammered *Shut up, Val. He's made it clear he doesn't want to talk.* But she needed to ensure that her mission was accom-

plished. He'd had her on a pedestal too long. She was
never the good-to-the-bone woman Sam thought her;
she was never some fragile, vulnerable victim but
someone who'd always caused her own problems—
and who hurt people in that wake.

"I wanted you to like them," she said clearly. "I
wanted you to see that they were good people. They
were older when they had me, but no daughter could
have been showered with more love. And they never,
ever tried to make me feel badly about any mistake I
made."

Sam said nothing, but he shot her a look. A deep,
dark, disbelieving look that she interpreted to mean
Do you really want to push a tiger? When his gaze
whipped back to the road, her palms were damp. But
she persisted.

"They were always good to me. When something
went wrong, it was always me, not them. Dad wanted
me to go into banking. I couldn't pass algebra. Mom
had major hopes that I'd be artistic. I couldn't draw a
straight line with a ruler. The antics I got into in
school . . . they never understood, but they were patient. And they never said a word of blame or judgment about my ex-husband, even though I was the one
who brought Ron into their lives and I know they were
hurt very badly—"

"Valentine?"

"Yes, Sam?" At least, she thought, he was talking.
The frustration emanating from his side of the car was
creating a packed bomb of an atmosphere. Better that
he let it out and get it off his chest.

"I think it's great. That you love your parents. But
I think, right now, that there isn't a prayer of a blue
moon that I could conceivably express how I feel

about your parents or this afternoon's outing without saying some things that you don't want to hear. Trust me, Red. Drop it for now."

For a while she did just that, staring straight ahead with a catch in her throat as thick as a stone. His response, truthfully, was exactly what she'd anticipated when she'd asked him on the outing. He'd been forced to see her in a more objective light, exactly what she felt had to happen. But still. She honestly hadn't wanted to upset him.

"I really embarrassed you, didn't I?"

The thought was in her mind. She wasn't aware she'd voiced it aloud until Sam jerked his head around and she got another of those piercing, thundercloud glares.

"Valentine?"

"Yes, Sam."

"I'm thinking right now of all the women I've known. Mothers, grandmothers, aunts, cousins, first dates, neighbors, high school crushes, lovers, friends. And of all the women—all those hundreds of women—I've never been even remotely inclined to shake any of them. Until you. I didn't even know I could *be* this mad at a woman. And I would gently advise you, Red, very very gently advise you, to never bring up the idea of your *embarrassing* me again."

Val opened her mouth to say a placating "Okay, Sam" and changed her mind. Silence seemed wiser. And what else was there to say? It was obvious that she'd gotten through. His attitude toward her had effectively undergone a metamorphosis. Sam radiated enough aggravated exasperation to fuel a furnace. He didn't look at her. And he sure as heck didn't want to touch her.

The drive was endless, the night ebony black when he pulled into her driveway. Val groped in her purse for the house key, then fumbled for something to say. It was a cinch that "thanks for coming with me, didn't we have fun" wasn't going to cut the mustard.

She managed, "You don't have to see me in, Sam."

But when she climbed out of the car, Sam was there, walking beside her to the porch, taking her key to unlock the door. He stepped in to flip on a light. It struck her eyes with the glare of a flashbulb. She was still wincing at the sudden brightness—she couldn't see his expression—when his lips grazed her cheek.

The tender gesture totally confused her, but he immediately backed away. "Look, I know you're tired. I'll lock up for you. Why don't you head straight for a shower and relax. There are things we need to communicate, clearly communicate, Valentine, but they'll wait."

They would wait, Val thought, because Sam didn't want to be anywhere around her right now. In fact, he probably wished he was miles away from a small town called Chekapee, and a woman he'd mistakenly thought was right for him.

She said a wooden good-night and turned around without another word. His suggestion of a shower gave her an easy excuse to disappear without any further awkward conversation. In minutes she was peeling off her clothes behind the closed bathroom door and trying not to feel a keening sense of loss.

After wrapping a towel around her hair, she stepped under the pelting hot shower spray. She didn't reach for the washcloth or soap. She just stood there under the liquid assault of water, with her eyes closed and her stomach clenched in knots. Familiar knots. She'd made mistakes before, had felt the same exact clenching guilt in her stomach before. But not this badly.

The mistakes she'd made in the past had never involved Sam.

Her skin was wrinkled when she flicked off the faucets. The whole bathroom was a warm, steamy cloud. Mindlessly she dried off and shimmied on her white silk nightgown. Her hair wasn't wet except for being damp at the temples. Still, unless she went through the ritual of a good brushing, it would be a tangled disaster in the morning. Judging from her ghostly reflection in the mirror, it was a tangled disaster now.

She opened the bathroom door with the brush in her hand. Exposure to the contrasting sudden cool air made her shiver. Yet once she flicked off the bathroom light, she completely forgot about the chill.

The house was dark, well, not exactly. Sam must have turned off the front-hall light when he left. But there was an odd glow of illumination coming from her bedroom, and she hadn't been in her bedroom yet. Unless she'd left a lamp burning that morning?

Confused, she padded down the hall. And then stopped.

Her bedroom drapes were drawn, her comforter pulled back to reveal cool, smooth sheets. She barely noticed those peripheral details. Her whole room was a fantasy of shadow, light and scent. The dozen candles on her round mirror table were all lit, pinpricks of flame that softly danced everywhere. The back of her closet door had a full-length mirror, where the candle flames were reflected a second time. And the long pewter-framed mirror over her chest of drawers echoed those soft teardrop flames again, so there seemed to be a hundred lit candles, and the heat of fire seduced their scents—vanilla, damask rose, lemon, hyacinth.

For an instant she saw herself in the dresser mirror, backdropped by candlelight, a small frozen figure in a short silk slip of a nightgown, barefoot, her hair looking as if it had been caught in a witch's wind, and the hairbrush in her hand suspended midair.

And then she saw Sam. Still fully clothed except that he was barefoot, like her, and his white shirt had been unbuttoned and pulled out of his slacks. His chest looked bronzed between the gaps of white cloth, and though he couldn't have grown a foot in the past half hour, he seemed to be at least seven feet tall in that candlelight. Tall. Dark, and rather unnervingly intimidating. His eyes reflected a darker, more primitive heat than any of the candles. And in that mirror, all that heat was focused on her.

"Now, don't get nervous, Valentine," he murmured.

"Nervous? I'm not nervous." Her heart was fluttering like dove's wings; her knees felt rickety and her throat was as dry as a cactus leaf. "Sam . . . I seem to have missed something fairly elemental here."

"That's no surprise. Honey, you've had a terrible day."

She motioned vaguely with the hairbrush. "The point is—I thought you left."

"I'm sure I never said I was leaving." Sam took the brush from her hand and moved behind her. "I told you I'd lock up. Which I did. And I suggested that you climb under a shower because you worked like a dog today, making everything go smoothly for your mother, and I knew you were tense. But I'm positive I never told you I was leaving. Close your eyes, Red. I'll take care of those tangles.''

She was far too bewildered to even think of closing her eyes. The last she knew—at least the last she *understood*—Sam didn't even want to be on the same planet with her. What he said about her mother made no sense. His *being* here made no sense.

And she watched him, behind her in the mirror, sift the brush through her hair. How many millions of times had she done the same thing? Hair was just...hair. Detangling the mop was a necessary chore, only Sam didn't seem to see it that way. She'd never pulled out a brush width and studied the texture and color under candle flames. She'd never let it fall, floating, drifting free, to rest just so on her bare shoulders. And she'd never, ever in her memory, shivered from the inside out from a simple hair brushing.

"I was going to cut it," she blurted out.

A crooked, wicked smile appeared in the mirror. "You'll have to walk over my dead body to get to the scissors."

"It's a pain. It frizzles up in humid weather and it's never been manageable this long and Shepherd, dammit, you're confusing me. You were *there*. You *know* nothing went smoothly at my mother's—"

"Yeah, it did. Because of you. You pitched in, picked up all the legwork chores, saved your mom from doing all the frazzle work. And your parents look at you like you're their ray of sunshine." Sam's voice turned whiskey rough. "Before I walked in that condo, I thought I had them all figured out. I figured them for pompous snobs. Higher-than-thou types, cruel, judgmental...and if they'd said one word to cut you down, I was prepared to level them. Foolishness. I should have known that nothing in life is ever that easy—put your head back, honey."

"Sam—"

"They love you."

"Shepherd—"

He tossed down the brush, used his fingertips to massage her scalp. "It's just that where I grew up, we expressed love differently. We talked. Sometimes we even yelled at each other, but the lines of communication were never closed. And I could see how it was with them. Hell, Red, they couldn't even ask you a simple question about how you were, because that would have risked hearing something about Chekapee. Ron, the bank, and Chekapee don't exist anymore, right? If something is uncomfortable, they just close the door—"

"Could I maybe get a word in here?"

"In a minute, Valentine. I could imagine how it was for you, growing up. Ask me, it's a good way to let hurts and fears and misunderstandings fester all out of proportion, if you're shut down every time you try to talk about them. Talk about a subtle way to cripple someone's confidence. But in the long run, Val, in the really long run, they're the losers. They're the ones who don't know how to connect. If you can't change them, you just have to move past letting it bother you—"

Val turned away from the mirror, turned toward him. Candlelight glowed in his eyes, as sensually incandescent as the real flames. Sam clearly wanted to lay all that philosophy on the table, but somehow she didn't think he'd come here to lecture her all night. Not the way he was looking at her. Her fingertips found his cheek. "Sam, I thought...I *really* thought...that you were mad at me."

He didn't mind changing to *that* subject. "I am."

"You're not acting, in any conceivable way, as if you were mad at me."

"That's how much you know. I'm not just *mad*— I'm downright furious with you for ever thinking you could be an embarrassment to me. The more I think about it, the madder I get. And there's a point, Valentine, where you'd better realize there are consequences when you push a man's temper over the edge."

Ten

Val felt the soft, slow stroke of his tongue on her throat. Wet. Warm. Intimate.

He'd warned her there were consequences for pushing a man's temper. Now she understood.

He nipped at the edge of her jaw, then wrapped his hands in her hair and found her mouth. The first kiss was lush and lazy, the second a dive into deeper waters. He sealed her lips with the seam of his, took her down, took her under. The problem with Sam, Val thought dizzily, was that he made her feel as if she were the only woman alive for him. It was just an illusion. A mesmerizing, delicious illusion. But he kissed her as if she were as precious as a rose petal, as needed as his own heartbeat. He kissed her as if she were part of him. He kissed her until she felt liquid from the inside out . . . and then he lifted his head.

"Strawberry suckers," he murmured whimsically. "Your mouth always reminds me of strawberry suckers." And then, the offhand announcement, "I'm gonna make you burn."

He spun her around, making the candle flames flicker and blur in the mirrors. Val, confused, had no idea why he would want her to face away from him. Until he said, "Look."

She shook her head.

"Yes. I want to see yourself...just like I see you. Look in the mirror, Valentine. Do it for me."

He was asking the impossible. She couldn't look at the woman exposed in the mirror's reflection; it made her feel too embarrassed, too painfully vulnerable. Her white nightgown was no more than a wisp of white silk held up by two thin straps, the light fabric revealing every flaw in her body. Sam's hand slid under a strap, slid down, his fingers disappearing from sight, stroking her breasts. The woman in the mirror sucked in her breath. Their eyes met, his without mercy.

"I want you to see that terrible woman in the mirror. I want you to see the bad, bad woman I've gotten myself involved with. I want you to see her...exactly like I see her."

Both his hands were in the mirror now. Her heartbeat thundered like a roar. Behind him, the room was a moving kaleidoscope of shadows and light. Her lace-edged pillows, the white carpet, the old Victorian furniture, the candle scents of vanilla and damask rose and sweet soft hyacinths...everything in the bedroom was feminine but him. His dark virility was striking, disturbing by contrast. His hands looked big and brown and masculine compared to her paler flesh.

He stroked the gown tight against her skin, so she could see her nipples, taut against the silk, see his hands roaming over her abdomen, then down, his palms riding intimately along the fronts of her thighs. The woman in the mirror... her skin flushed, and as if her neck was weak, her head fell back against him.

She whispered, "Let me turn around, Sam."

"Not yet."

He pulled the silky fabric up, up, over her head. When the nightgown was gone, her hair drifted back down in clouds, russet-red clouds that covered her shoulders and almost reached the tips of her breasts. Almost. Her hair wasn't long enough to conceal anything that mattered, and his big hands cupped her breasts, showing them off to her in the mirror.

"They ache, don't they." His voice was as seductive and slow as bourbon and blues. "They feel heavy and hot in my hands. I want you to know that it *embarrasses* me, Valentine, the way you respond to me. Your skin gets this glow and your eyes turn all liquid and sleepy. I hate it, honey. Your nipples get all tight and tiny when I touch them a certain way. I really hate that. And when you start shivering... you should be ashamed, Val. I want you to be ashamed, to feel *worried*, about how much you're embarrassing me—"

A sound tore out of her throat, nothing stronger than the crack of a broken whisper. She whipped around.

"I'm gonna strangle you, Shepherd."

The threat didn't seem to scare him, possibly because there was far more tremble than threat in her voice. And he didn't try to run, she noticed, when she started pushing the shirt off his shoulders. "You think I'm beautiful," she accused him.

"Sweetheart, that's not news."

The shirt caught at his cuffs. She had to wrestle it past the buttons. When it was finally free, she hurled the blasted thing at the floor. "I don't embarrass you."

"Never would. Never could," he affirmed.

"I've made terrible mistakes, Sam. I've told you. I've shown you. How come I can't get through?"

"Maybe you always got through. Maybe I was never looking for a perfect saint of a woman. Maybe the only thing I ever wanted was a hellion, and, love, you've got enough fire in your eyes to burn me up right now. If you want to talk, it's going to be later." He added, "Much later."

He scooped her up as if she weighed no more than thistledown. The mattress springs creaked when he dropped her in the center of the bed. He took only enough time to yank down the zipper and kick off his pants before following.

Her arms were open, waiting. If he wanted a hellion, Val thought, he was gonna get one. Her heart felt the battering of a thousand conflicting emotions. It was Sam's fault she was out of control. All Sam's fault. From the day she'd met him, the damn man mixed her up until she couldn't see straight. He forced her to relook at her life and everything she'd always taken for granted. He didn't see anything the way she did. He'd worried her and upset her and shaken her up.

And now, he was going to pay.

Their lips fused in the tantalizing drug of an open-mouthed kiss. She tasted urgency and impatience, on his tongue, on hers. Flames and shadows played on his bronze skin, and the feel of him, length to length, made her pulse thrum with a dizzying, distracting anticipation. In two seconds, he could be inside her. He was more than ready. So was she.

But she tore free from his arms and twisted until she was kneeling. When Sam reached for her, she gently pushed his hands aside. It was pay-up time for Mr. Carson Samuel Shepherd. In a slow-motion frenzy she kissed the hard slope, the lean muscle of his shoulder, his chest, his flat smooth abdomen.

In moments the only sounds in the room were the hiss of candles and Sam's ragged breathing and the rub-and-slide sounds of her hands on his skin. She wanted him to ache. She wanted him to know how beautiful she found *his* body. She wanted him to feel the same wonder, the same melting need, the same confusing and powerful desire he made *her* feel. And when he was aching so badly that he couldn't stand it, she wanted to make him ache some more.

She kissed. She touched. She found . . . discoveries. He was ticklish behind his knees. The inside of his thigh...he went crazy when she touched him there. He liked the soft stroke of her hands on his throat, the feel of her knuckles in the small of his back. Absorbed, her discoveries became more intimate. When her palm circled the most vulnerable part of him, she felt the pulse of blood surge just beneath the soft-hard steel. Afraid of hurting him, she more carefully ran her fingertips down the veins and ridges, over the smooth warm tip. He bucked again.

Worried now that she was doing something wrong, she shot a peek at Sam's face. His profile was averted away from her. Realizing where he was focusing, she turned her head.

Their eyes met in the bureau mirror, where he'd been watching...watching her kiss him, watching her touch him, watching the emotions play on her face as the flames flickered and shone on her bare skin. Val swallowed. His eyes were a lustrous blaze. In his eyes, she really was beautiful. In his eyes...oh, God, the depth of love she saw in his eyes made her gulp a second time.

"My hellion," he whispered, "loves me."

"You knew that. I told you—"

"I know what you told me. But I wasn't sure how you really felt. You've been fighting me harder than a cat in a cage. Putting up brick walls faster than I could tear them down. And I have to warn you, honey. If this is what happens when I lose my temper, I'm probably gonna lose my temper with you every day of our lives."

He'd layered her beneath him before he stopped teasing, and there was no teasing after that next kiss. They'd made love before, but this was different. As different as the glitter of fool's gold and the real thing. As different as mating and the elemental joining of two souls. He took the time to protect her, the same way, Val thought, Sam would always assume the basic right to protect the woman he loved.

She saw it in his face, in the way he touched her, in the way he took her...that he believed this night was a taste of the future. Knowing—*believing*—she loved him made a difference. The fences were down. Boundaries torn away. And the real power of his love exposed, huge, generous, limitless, free to be expressed.

For a single, brief second, she was afraid. It was a commitment from her soul he wanted. A commitment from her soul he assumed.

Yet the love in his eyes burned away that momentary fear. And the music...his body made music to hers, made her blood heat thick and rich, made her limbs dip and sway to match his rhythm. Her breath spun like a satin ribbon, unraveling her emotions and reducing them to sheer feminine instinct. She'd been an empty well. He filled her. She'd been joyless. He gave her back that joy in herself.

And her vulnerable heart opened to him, because he gave her no choice. There was simply nothing she could deny Sam.

When Val opened her eyes the next morning, the first thing she saw was Sam's face on the pillow next to her. His hair was all rumpled, his chin had a whisker stubble, and he was sleeping like the dead. At some point near dawn he'd turned over on his stomach, but beneath the covers, his hand was nestled in hers. Pretty corny, she thought, to have fallen asleep holding hands after the cataclysmic passion they'd shared.

But it didn't feel corny. It felt...right. So right that her heart filled with an ocean of emotion, vast and huge and consuming. On the mirrored table, the candles had all burned down, but their scents still lingered in the room, invoking memories of the night before. She'd done things with Sam that, once, she thought no good woman would do with a man. With him, nothing seemed wrong. With him, a hundred things she always thought were terribly wrong had a dangerous tendency to seem terribly right.

Sleepily, thoughtfully, she considered how she could possibly have fallen in love with such a dreadful man. He'd gotten her drunk to find out her secrets. He'd lied to her—about money, about caring, about anything he pleased—whatever it took to keep her from sending him away. He was nice to Lincoln, to Jonesey, to the sheriff, to everyone in town. Everyone but her. He was devious and tricky with her, and he'd outright broken laws to find a way to sneak money into her till, and the worst. He'd ruthlessly battered at the insecurities she'd been carrying around her whole life.

It was a lot to go through, for a woman he couldn't be sure of winning. For a woman, who Val had been trying to convince him from the start, wasn't worth it.

She raised up on an elbow, intending to lean over and kiss him, when with a shock she noticed the clock. The dial read five after nine. The store should have been open five minutes ago. Jonesey wasn't due in today, and on the day after Thanksgiving, the shopping district should be flooded with customers.

She kissed him, softly, swiftly, a tender brush on his cheek that never woke him. Just as gently, reluctantly, she unfolded her fingers from his. And then bounded out of bed.

In the closet, she thumbed past all the navy blues and demure grays. Without needing to think, she tossed an emerald skirt on the chair, a skirt short enough to show off her legs and snug enough to show off her behind. Then a blouse with bright jewel colors. She slipped on slinky underwear, then sprinted to the bathroom for a washup and makeup, then back to the bedroom to finish dressing.

Sam didn't waken. She raced around again—there was no time for coffee and breakfast—but she needed to gather a purse and shoes. When she peeked in the bedroom doorway one last time, he still hadn't stirred.

Val hesitated. He'd realize that she was at the store, but it still seemed wrong to leave without saying something, especially after last night. There was so much she wanted to say. So much she'd neglected to say to Sam for so long.

On the other hand, to wake him up seemed purely selfish. She knew—she intimately knew—the reason he was so exhausted.

She'd let him sleep, she decided, and call him from the store just as soon as she could.

Lincoln was waiting for her when she reached the store, hanging out at the door with a worried frown on his face and his hands jammed in fists in his jeans pockets.

"Come on in, Linc. What's wrong?" She unlocked the door and let them both in.

"You know a few days ago, when Sam took me for ice cream and we were riding around in the Mustang with the top down?" Linc dogged her footsteps as she whisked around opening up. "Well, Sam told me to talk to you. He said to just ask it, straight out. I mean like you and me, Val, we stick together. I don't want to do anything to mess that up, you know? So the question I gotta ask is whether you and me would still be friends if I wasn't working for you."

Val stopped whisking around and gave her young friend her full attention. "We made a pact about being friends for life, didn't we? As far as I'm concerned, kiddo, we'll always be friends. And that has nothing to do with whether you're working for me."

"You sure?"

"I'm sure."

Linc released a huge relieved sigh. "'Cause my mom's got a guy, see. He's pretty nice, gave her a ring and all. His name's Jim. He's got a daughter—a real pain—she's only four, but he told me he always wanted a son. He took me fishing and stuff. Where he works, he gets off at three, and he's been fixing stuff at the house—I guess they're getting married, that's sure all they're talking about—anyway, he kind of wants me to hang around more. A lot of times, we're stuck taking the pain around with us, but it's kinda fun, fixing stuff with him, and like I told him about the job I had, taking care of you and all, and he understands about a man's responsibilities, but—"

Val tactfully released him from those responsibilities, feeling warmed to the bone that something was finally going right in her young friend's life. When Linc left the store, she noticed it was past ten-thirty. She quickly headed straight for the phone behind the counter to call Sam, but never reached it. The bell over the door jangled. Then jangled again.

Customers filled the store before she could blink. On one of the heaviest shopping days of the year, Val had expected customers, but she'd expected her regulars and some strangers and early Christmas shoppers. Not people she hadn't seen in years. And all of them, Val thought, were behaving unbelievably strangely.

Right behind a group of giggling preteens, Mabel Summers strode up to the cash register with an armload of books. Mabel ran the Lazy Day Motel where Sam was staying. She hadn't once patronized the store from the day it opened.

"It's nice to see you," Val said politely.

"Yes, well . . ." Mabel nervously tugged on her ear-lobe and took a breath. "I saw your car in the motel parking lot the other day. And I started to think, your mother isn't in town. In fact, you don't have any family in town, and . . ."

Val waited, unsure what was coming.

Mabel tried again. "I took one look at Sam and thought he was nice, you understand. Adorable with those big brown eyes and all, but honey . . ."

Val waited again, becoming more confused. The older woman was clearly nervous and uncomfortable, and her tone reeked of meaningful undertones.

"I was just remembering, Valerie, when Weber Johnson got you in trouble. You remember, you couldn't have been twelve, and Weber talked you into climbing the church bell tower, and the next thing we all knew that bell was ringing on a Tuesday night. He'd locked you in and taken off. You remember, how he took off on you?"

Val nodded, she remembered, and then cocked her head expectantly. She'd heard Weber Johnson had a job at the air strip. She assumed Mabel was going to tell her there was some link to Sam.

But no. Mabel started to say something else, looked at her, and then sighed heavily. "Here," she said defeatedly, and shoved the stack of books toward the cash register. "I just wanted to bring you business, is all."

"Well, thank you," Val said, totally bewildered by the entire exchange.

It was noon before she had the chance to call home, but there was no answer at her house. She dialed Sam's motel room, but the phone rang a dozen times without an answer there, too. When she picked up the phone for a third time to ring his store, all six raw-boned feet of polyester-clad Miss Holmes was striding toward her. Miss Holmes, who never gave her the time of day if she could help it. Miss Holmes, carrying a toppling pile of science fiction paperbacks that were all tangled up with her purse and the strap of her glasses.

"Let me help you," Val said.

Once Miss Holmes's glasses were saved and the books neatly stacked on the counter, Val started punching in the amounts.

"I was just thinking, Valerie, that you are the only one I know who never made fun of my love for science fiction."

Val paused. "Everyone's entitled to read for fun, don't you think?"

"Fun, yes." Miss Holmes pushed her glasses higher on her nose. "I was also remembering, Valerie, a certain boy who used to pass you notes in my senior English class. In trouble with the law, that boy. I always had my eye on him. I forget his name, but he followed you around like a puppy. You were nice to him, when all the other girls had enough sense to brush him off. But there is a time, my dear, when a woman simply *must be* tough."

Val thought, I've entered the twilight zone and any minute now I'm going to wake up. "Is there some reason you're bringing up Tommy Walker after all this time?" she asked delicately.

"Only as a general reference to men." Miss Holmes sniffed. "When I was younger, I had my share of men come calling. Believe me, I *know* men. The male of the species is simply not predictable, Valerie, and especially the good-looking ones. You were always too trusting, my dear. There could be,'' she said meaningfully, ''a viper right under your nose. One must be tough. And if one isn't tough, one must *learn* to be tough.''

''I...um...thank you for that advice, Miss Holmes.''

For a brief stretch the store was quiet after that. Val found herself drumming her fingers on the counter, at first amused by the whole conversation and then, simply, confused. Neither Mabel nor Miss Holmes had willingly talked with her since the debacle with Ron. She was delighted to be off their enemy list and buoyed to be treated like a neighbor again. Only their change in attitude was certainly sudden, and their choice of conversational topics straight off-the-wall.

Restlessly she paced to the window. Predictably shoppers were milling down the street. A few clouds polka-dotted the pale blue sky. Kids raced past, jackets hanging open. Mothers followed, juggling parcels and purses. Val had seen the familiar scene a hundred times.

But something unusual seemed to be happening across the street. In Martha Witherspoon's bakery, Val noticed quite a crowd through the dusty window. Not a usual crowd, but a bustling clutch of people. Val blinked. Some woman slammed her fist on the glass counter above the doughnut shelf. Whatever they were talking about in there, the gossip must be pretty heated.

Something is going on, she thought, and was suddenly, totally conscious of not caring. It was still her hometown. Heaven knew, she'd struggled hard to fit in, worked hard for acceptance. But there was a time that everything happening in Chekapee had desperately mattered to her.

Now the only thing that desperately mattered to her was connecting with Sam. She crossed behind the counter again and reached for the phone. She tried the store, the house, his motel room.

No Sam.

Then she tried them all a second time.

Still no Sam.

An uneasy shiver chased up her spine. There was no reason, she told herself, to think that anything was wrong. He could be anywhere. A million places. She would see him at dinner if she couldn't catch him sooner. It was just... there were things she wished she'd said last night, this morning.

There were things she *should* have said to Sam a long time ago.

And possibly the whole crazy day was affecting her, but she couldn't seem to shake the feeling that something was seriously wrong.

Eleven

Sam heard the phone ring several times. He let it ring. Every retail establishment on River Street was bustling today except for his. His blinds were still drawn; the Closed sign still facing the street, the door still locked.

Val wanted him to shut the place down.

He was shutting it down.

Dismantling the sucker took more nuisance running around than actual work. The rented cash register had to be returned. His volunteer help had to be called and canceled. He had to find a home for the bricks and plywood that had worked as temporary shelving. Somebody had donated the card table and chairs; they had to be taken back. He needed to call Florida Power and Light and the phone company to cancel services.

At three in the afternoon, Sam popped the lid on a soda pop and took a long thirsty gulp. The blasted chores were finished. He dropped down to the dusty floor, bent his knees and leaned his head against the bare wall. There was nothing left in the store but cardboard boxes of books, Val's books, which couldn't be returned until after hours. Basically, though, his midnight marauding was done.

The thought terrified him. Sam took another gulp of pop. Running around all day hadn't helped. He'd woken up in a state of anxiety, and his pulse rate was still locked in a thrumming panic zone. Once the store was put out of commission, he'd run out of excuses to stay in Chekapee.

Last night he remembered teasing Val about the future. And now he remembered, like a knife twist in his heart, that she hadn't answered.

The telephone rang again. He ignored it, unwilling to take any chances that the caller was Val. When he woke up that morning and found her gone, he understood that she'd left for work. But his first response had been a coward's relief. A showdown—a serious showdown about their future—was inevitable. But tonight, Sam thought, was soon enough. The anxiety gnawing his nerves all day had the obvious source. If he hadn't won her by now—he damn well had to face it—he'd lost.

He had no desire to risk hearing that until he had to.

Outside, he heard footsteps clicking by, cars honking, the muted drift of some pedestrian's laughter. The sounds of her town were familiar by now. Sam shook his head in frustration. There was a time he thought this town was her enemy, but that wasn't true. Val wasn't attached to Chekapee. She wasn't attached to her damned bookstore. The only thing that brought her back here, the only thing keeping her here, was something she thought she had to prove. About self-worth. About living down old ghosts.

His redhead had to believe in herself. And Sam knew that real confidence had to come from within. But he'd thought—he'd really, really believed—that if he loved her enough, it would make a difference.

God, Val was the best thing that ever happened to him. Fear of losing her made him ache from the inside out. She fit him, as no other woman had. She *knew* him as no other woman had. When he put on a smile for the world, the world believed his smile. Not Val. She knew when he was blue, knew when he was cross, knew he hated feeling vulnerable and somehow she even made that all right. At a deep gut level, his redhead had taught him about real trust, simply by never being less than totally honest with him. She made him laugh. She turned him on until he couldn't see straight. She challenged him to think, to feel. When they were together, they made a planet of two.

It wasn't going to take any courage, tonight, to ask her to marry him.

But Sam was afraid it took more courage than he had, to risk her saying no.

When Val drove in around six, Sam was fresh-shaved, fresh-showered, fresh-combed and as primed as a pressure pump. Worrying was the pits. He'd spent the past eight hours living in that limbo, and he was through with negative thinking. They needed to communicate clearly, honestly, and he was ready.

Val clipped up the porch steps just as he opened the door. "Sam! I've been trying to reach you all day! I felt terrible about leaving you this morning—"

"Hey, it's okay. I knew you had to be at the store."
One look, and his optimism skittered like an uneasy
colt. He couldn't keep his eyes off her. She looked so
beautiful. Beautiful . . . but different.

She'd worn her hair down and loose and flowing
around her shoulders. Only she never—ever—wore
her hair down to work. And she peeled off her raincoat, revealing a sassy little skirt and a soft blouse in
a million colors that showed off her slim figure. He
liked the clothes and he loved the way she looked in
them, but he didn't know what all those changes
meant.

Worst of all, there was something new in her eyes.
Something bold and bright and determined in the way
Val looked at him. "We need to talk, love," she said
softly.

Exactly what Sam had been thinking all day, but
abruptly faced with truth or consequences, he could
almost hear the anxiety sluicing through his pulse. "I
know we need to talk. And I want to talk, too. But
you've been working all day. How about if we relax
and have some dinner first? I'll cook." He headed
straight for the kitchen at a near jog.

"Shepherd?"

"What?"

"Could you slow down long enough to kiss me
hello?"

He slowed down, but his heartbeat didn't. It was
pretty damn ridiculous, feeling terrified to kiss her
after all the intimacies they'd shared. But he just
didn't want to do anything, say anything, act any way
wrong that could tip the scales against him. With a
slow smile, he angled down and brushed her lips with
the care and caution he'd treat an explosive chemical.

He lifted his head with another smile. Hers was gone. She suddenly looked . . . hurt.

"God. What's wrong?" he said.

"Nothing," she said swiftly, and hurriedly changed subjects. "I've had the strangest, oddest day."

It was better, Sam thought, when they moved in the kitchen. She wouldn't sit—though he argued with her—so he chopped salad while she fussed, browning potatoes. Although he was careful not to point it out, they were acting just like married people, bumping hips, opening and closing cupboards while they debated dinner. He broiled chicken on the grill with lemon pepper. She made a fancy sauce to pour onto the broccoli. A simple dessert. Fresh fruits, cut up just so. By the time it was all ready, the table looked like a feast.

Only neither of them was eating. She kept looking at him. He kept looking back. Then she'd pick up her fork and nibble something. He'd try to swallow a spoonful of something else. She kept trying to hold a conversation . . . she'd had *customers* that day, not just strangers stopping off the street, but the old friends and neighbors who'd been shunning her all this time.

Sam was hard-pressed to concentrate. Her customers, after all, were hardly a surprise. He'd been feeding clues to the town for weeks that he was a bastard, all too similar to the jerk they'd mistakenly trusted before. From there it was only a hop-skip for them to recognize that their enemy was not, and never had been, Valentine. "Honey, you were never more than a scapegoat for the hard feelings they were carrying for your ex. They were never really mad at you."

"They had a right to be mad."

"Not at you."

"I felt responsible, Sam."

"I know you did. And expect you still do. It's not something you can break overnight, this habit you have of being hard on yourself."

She set down her fork and clasped her hands in her lap. Her eyes rested on his face with disquieting intensity. "There were a lot of habits I was trying to break when I met you in the Gulf. In fact, I thought I had the sense to swear off men until I had my life together."

Alarm pulsed through his whole body. He said smoothly, "I don't think it works that way. That you can pick a day when your whole house is dusted and the guy will just be there."

"Sam . . . I know that now. I—"

Sam clawed to his feet so rapidly that all the dishes rattled. "I can see that you're not hungry. And you've been on your feet all day. How about if you take a nice soothing soak in the tub—I'll just whip away the dishes—and then we'll talk. We'll really talk."

She stared at him in bewilderment. "I'm really *not* tired—"

"Sure, you are."

"And I really *don't* want a bath—"

"Sure, you do. Think how great that warm water will feel. Think how good an old pair of sweats or a robe will feel after being in working clothes all day. And by the time you get out of the bath, I'll have the food and the dishes taken care of."

Val hesitated, obviously wanting to protest again, but then she searched his face and changed her mind. The instant she disappeared down the hall, Sam raked a hand through his hair. He'd completely changed his mind about the need for any showdown. Living in limbo wasn't so bad. He could wait. There were more things he could do, more things he could try. Maybe he could have thirty pounds of Godiva chocolate shipped from Europe in the shape of a giant valentine. Maybe he could hook a banner to the King Air that read *Marry me Val,* and fly it back and forth across Chekapee every day until he wore her down. Maybe...

The doorbell rang. Sam hadn't shoved the chicken in the refrigerator and straightened before someone jabbed the bell a second time. Wiping his hands on a kitchen towel, he strode toward the foyer with a glance down the hall—Val was closed up in the bathroom. The bell pealed yet again.

Impatiently he yanked the door open. His mouth opened, too, and then abruptly closed.

There had to be a dozen people jammed on her front porch, and cars were parked every which way past her driveway and down the street. He recognized most of the faces. Jane Shraver, Mabel from the motel, the bat, the elderly Martha Witherspoon, Mrs. Gatchell, Sue Ellen. All the women who'd once greeted him with friendly smiles were distinctly not smiling now. They were mad. Foot-stomping, scowling, loud-voices mad. At him.

Sam sucked in his breath. The "lynch mob" was almost entirely composed of buxom dowagers, so fear never crossed his mind—but hindsight sure did. He'd always known there was a teensy potential repercussion to his propaganda campaign. What it took to get the townspeople to see Val as an innocent victim, unfortunately, was to give them an identifiable enemy. He'd been willing. He'd been handy. He was the one who could possibly fill that role. And it was hard to regret what he'd done when the measure of his success was the number of people here now.

At that precise instant, though, he'd sure rather be in Poughkeepsie.

"I told you it was his car parked here! Parked here all last night, too. I told you all!" One woman's voice raised in the crowd, then another, directed at him, "*Where* is Valerie?"

"She's here. She's fine. Just take it easy, everybody. If you'll all calm down and listen to me a minute—"

A less-than-popular suggestion, Sam noticed. He heard the low rumble of displeasure. Bodies crowded closer. A finger stabbed in his chest. "You look here, Shepherd. You're a Northerner and a con artist, just like that Ron, thought he could fool all of us and get away with it. Well, we've got news for you. You think we don't know your kind, we do. You didn't trick any of us, not for one minute—"

"Valerie's one of ours, and in this town we protect our own—"

"Rose Wilkins here, she's tearing up your lease. You don't have a business in Chekapee anymore. You just head right back north where you belong. There's nothing lower on earth than a worm who'd prey on a vulnerable woman—"

"What on earth is going on here?" Val had bolted out of the tub the minute she heard the noisy commotion. Now, hugging a robe closed over her still-damp skin, she surged through the sea of bodies. The look on her neighbors' faces stunned her. Without needing to think, she sidestepped in front of Sam like David protecting Goliath. "Why are you all here? What's going on?"

Everyone began talking at once.

"You listen to us, Valerie. He isn't what he seems—"

"He's been stealing your business, that's what he's been doing. And when Sue Ellen saw his car parked

outside your house all last night, we figured he'd
conned you into something else. He's no good, we're
telling you, Valerie—"

"Took us for fools, he did. Just like that Ron. And
you may not have kinfolk in town, but you've got us,
and we're not about to see another snake in the grass
hurt you again. Just step aside, Valerie. We're more
than capable of taking care of that bas—"

Val interrupted in a clear, strong voice. "That's it.
This has gone far enough. You're all coming from
some major misunderstandings if you could possibly
think Sam is anything like Ron. You're simply wrong.
And I won't tolerate anyone name-calling the man I'm
going to marry."

The word *marry* affected the crowd like the air fiz-
zling out of a balloon. Jaws hung open. Harsh glares
turned to frowns of total confusion. The announcement was so clearly unexpected.

"Marry," she repeated, with her back still to Sam.
At that moment, to save her life, she couldn't have
looked at his face. The word had slipped out of her
lips on impulse. She could have sworn—*sworn*—that
she'd outgrown that dreadful impetuous tendency to
say things on impulse. Worse yet, more impulsive
words tumbled out before she could stop them. "Sam
asked me to marry him last night, and I said yes. This
was no quick decision—we've loved each other for a
long time—but we had a lot of serious plans to work
out. Basically we're going to live in Chicago—that's
where his work is. And I talked with Jonesey late this
afternoon—Bartholomew is going to take over the
store."

Her calm, rational voice seemed to communicate
assurance. The last of the heat seeped out of the
crowd. But one voice piped up, "Valerie, something

really *is* confused here. We didn't know he cared about you. From what everyone said about things he'd done..."

"No one knows better than I do how misunderstandings blow out of proportion, how mistakes can get blown out of proportion if you listen to what everyone says." Val moved forward, which effectively started the slow exodus off her porch. "I appreciate your concern. I appreciate your caring. But whatever the misunderstanding—I know Sam. Really know him. And there's no problem here that you need to worry about."

It was another twenty minutes before the last hanger-on left the porch and drove away. In the sudden silence, Val turned around, her stomach still flip-flopping with nerves. In a thousand years, she'd never expected that crowd of ex-neighbors and friends to come—however misguided their motives—in support of her.

It struck her as equally strange that a strong, six-foot man who could charm a sucker from a baby hadn't said a single word in his own defense. Or attempted a word of explanation. Or responded in any way to the startling—some might say astounding—claim that he'd asked her to marry him. And Sam was nowhere in sight.

She found him in the kitchen. Wrapping cellophane in copious amounts around the broccoli that neither of them had eaten. The rest of the dishes were already stacked in the dishwasher. Sam was so busy with domestic chores that he couldn't even look at her.

Or didn't want to look at her?

Val tucked her arms under her chest, defensively tight, desperately wishing she could fathom his mind. His reaction to their unexpected visitors was one thing, but Sam had been like a total stranger since she'd walked in before dinner. Distant. Tense. And as jumpy as the trigger on a time bomb.

Whatever was wrong had to come out, but she fumbled for the right thing to say. It seemed logical to start with what just happened. "My heart's still thumping," she confessed. "When I saw all those people outside, I was all shook up. I had no idea what was going on. It was . . . um . . . flustering."

"Quite a scene out there," Sam agreed.

"And I thought it kind of odd," she continued conversationally, "that you didn't say anything . . . didn't even seem to look surprised. It was almost as if you expected them to show up. I don't suppose that you might have done something that I don't know about? Something that may have specifically triggered all those sweet-faced ladies into thinking you were a rat?"

"You have to be kidding. What could I possibly have done?"

"Sam?"

"Yes, honey."

"Put down that silly pot holder and look at me."

He put down the silly pot holder. And he looked at her. Val thought he'd smile. Instead, the sheer agony of anxiety in his eyes came perilously close to giving her a heart attack. Chekapee's coffee klatch of gossipers certainly hadn't put that look in his eyes. Sam was scared. Sam, who would lie, cheat, steal, mow bulldozers down in his path and do anything he had to do—without a qualm of conscience—for something he believed in. Sam, who was scared of nothing.

Except, maybe, her. Val thought about how willingly, how openly he'd laid his heart on the line for her. With no guarantee of a return.

Clearly that situation had to be immediately corrected.

"What I did or didn't do doesn't matter," he said. "They came out to protect you, Valentine. They came out shouting for you. Does that tell you how this town really feels about you?" He picked up a dishcloth.

"I don't give a damn how anybody feels about me. Except for you." She took the dishcloth out of his hands and hurled it. He blinked in surprise. And blinked again when she waggled a finger under his nose. "You kissed me like a *sister* when I first walked in, Shepherd. You wouldn't talk to me. You shuttled me off to the bathtub like you were postponing the moment when you had to drink castor oil. You scared me to *death,* and now if you think you're gonna make a liar out of me—"

"A liar?"

He liked her scolding him. Val could see it. He'd always liked it when she showed a brassy, sassy confidence, and the drawn lines on his face were already easing. She advanced on him, waggling her finger again. "You heard what I said in front of all those people. Well? Are you going to marry me or not?"

She watched him reach back. His hand encountered the smooth surface of the refrigerator. Sam, once, had cornered her in the bookstore using suspiciously similar tactics, which he seemed to realize. His gaze hadn't budged from her face, but at least that terrible look of uncertainty was gone.

"Ah...Red? Are you playing with me?"

"You bet I am. The same way I intend to play with you for the rest of our lives. You're the one who taught me how to play down and dirty, no holds barred, no rules...except the rules that work for us. You'd better be good and scared, Sam, because you *are* going to get what's coming to you.''

Her voice, of its own volition, lowered to a throaty whisper. And a nice big lump chugged down his Adam's apple when her fingers splayed on his chest and slowly, possessively, started climbing. Still, he took a cautious breath. ''All those nuptial plans you mentioned to the crowd, Valentine . . . that could have been something you were just saying. On impulse. Because, like you said, you were flustered.''

''True. But that won't get you off the hook.'' Her fingertip flipped open one button on his shirt. Then a second button. And for the first time all evening, she saw his mouth start to curl in a slow, slow smile. ''You already know I'm impulsive. You already know about every mistake I ever made. You set a bad precedent in loving me for myself, faults and all. And now you pay the price, because I'm not letting you go. Is that perfectly clear?''

She meant to keep talking, because Sam seemed to gain confidence and assurance the longer she teased him. But the teasing . . . it was hard to keep up.

His skin was warm against her hands. Warm and mobile. When she laced her arms around his neck, the electricity between them could have powered the planet. That kind of power was a serious business. Belonging . . . she could taste the rightness of it. His eyes deepened to the color of rich, dark chocolate, and so gently, he stroked back a strand of her hair.

''There was a time,'' he murmured, ''when I thought it was a big deal to you. Your worry about disappointing me.''

''I certainly tried worrying about that. I tried my best,'' she whispered. ''But I discovered that's an awfully tough attitude to hang on to, when the man you love continually acts proud of you.''

"Me? You think I'm proud of you? Just because you've had a rough road, and you tackled your dragons head-on? Just because I think you have more courage and honesty than anyone I've ever known? Just because doing something that's hard is never going to stop you? Just because you're the best woman I've ever known?''

She said softly, "I love you from here to forever, Sam.''

"Do you have any...*any*...idea how much I love you?''

So fierce his eyes. So fierce and vulnerable with love. She went up on tiptoe and pulled his head down. She knew well how much he loved her...and how much difference it had made in her life. She planned to make that kind of wonderful difference in his.

She gave him a kiss, a promise of the future. And then took a kiss, a promise of the future, as well.

Sometime much later Sam said, "Yes", as if that covered any question he might have forgotten to answer.

Val thought the single word said it all.

* * * * *

OFFICIAL RULES • MILLION DOLLAR MATCH 3 SWEEPSTAKES
NO PURCHASE OR OBLIGATION NECESSARY TO ENTER

To enter, follow the directions published. **ALTERNATE MEANS OF ENTRY:** Hand print your name and address on a 3″ ×5″ card and mail to either: Silhouette "Match 3," 3010 Walden Ave., P.O. Box 1867, Buffalo, NY 14269-1867, or Silhouette "Match 3," P.O. Box 609, Fort Erie, Ontario L2A 5X3, and we will assign your Sweepstakes numbers. (Limit: one entry per envelope.) For eligibility, entries must be received no later than March 31, 1994. No responsibility is assumed for lost, late or misdirected entries.

Upon receipt of entry, Sweepstakes numbers will be assigned. To determine winners, Sweepstakes numbers will be compared against a list of randomly preselected prizewinning numbers. In the event all prizes are not claimed via the return of prizewinning numbers, random drawings will be held from among all other entries received to award unclaimed prizes.

Prizewinners will be determined no later than May 30, 1994. Selection of winning numbers and random drawings are under the supervision of D.L. Blair, Inc., an independent judging organization, whose decisions are final. One prize to a family or organization. No substitution will be made for any prize, except as offered. Taxes and duties on all prizes are the sole responsibility of winners. Winners will be notified by mail. Chances of winning are determined by the number of entries distributed and received.

Sweepstakes open to persons 18 years of age or older, except employees and immediate family members of Torstar Corporation, D.L. Blair, Inc., their affiliates, subsidiaries and all other agencies, entities and persons connected with the use, marketing or conduct of this Sweepstakes. All applicable laws and regulations apply. Sweepstakes offer void wherever prohibited by law. Any litigation within the province of Quebec respecting the conduct and awarding of a prize in this Sweepstakes must be submitted to the Régies des Loteries et Courses du Quebec. In order to win a prize, residents of Canada will be required to correctly answer a time-limited arithmetical skill-testing question. Values of all prizes are in U.S. currency.

Winners of major prizes will be obligated to sign and return an affidavit of eligibility and release of liability within 30 days of notification. In the event of non-compliance within this time period, prize may be awarded to an alternate winner. Any prize or prize notification returned as undeliverable will result in the awarding of that prize to an alternate winner. By acceptance of their prize, winners consent to use of their names, photographs or other likenesses for purposes of advertising, trade and promotion on behalf of Torstar Corporation without further compensation, unless prohibited by law.

This Sweepstakes is presented by Torstar Corporation, its subsidiaries and affiliates in conjunction with book, merchandise and/or product offerings. Prizes are as follows: Grand Prize—$1,000,000 (payable at $33,333.33 a year for 30 years). First through Sixth Prizes may be presented in different creative executions, each with the following approximate values: First Prize—$35,000; Second Prize—$10,000; 2 Third Prizes—$5,000 each; 5 Fourth Prizes—$1,000 each; 10 Fifth Prizes—$250 each; 1,000 Sixth Prizes—$100 each. Prizewinners will have the opportunity of selecting any prize offered for that level. A travel-prize option, if offered and selected by winner, must be completed within 12 months of selection and is subject to hotel and flight accommodations availability. Torstar Corporation may present this Sweepstakes utilizing names other than Million Dollar Sweepstakes. For a current list of all prize options offered within prize levels and all names the Sweepstakes may utilize, send a self-addressed, stamped envelope (WA residents need not affix return postage) to: Million Dollar Sweepstakes Prize Options/Names, P.O. Box 4710, Blair,[fj NE 68009.

The Extra Bonus Prize will be awarded in a random drawing to be conducted no later than May 30, 1994 from among all entries received. To qualify, entries must be received by March 31, 1994 and comply with published directions. No purchase necessary. For complete rules, send a self-addressed, stamped envelope (WA residents need not affix return postage) to: Extra Bonus Prize Rules, P.O. Box 4600, Blair, NE 68009.

For a list of prizewinners (available after July 31, 1994) send a separate, stamped, self-addressed envelope to: Million Dollar Sweepstakes Winners, P.O. Box 4728, Blair, NE 68009.   SWP-1292

Experience the beauty of Yuletide romance with Silhouette Christmas Stories 1992—a collection of heartwarming stories by favorite Silhouette authors.

JONI'S MAGIC by Mary Lynn Baxter
HEARTS OF HOPE by Sondra Stanford
THE NIGHT SANTA CLAUS RETURNED by Marie Ferrarrella
BASKET OF LOVE by Jeanne Stephens

Also available this year are three popular early editions of Silhouette Christmas Stories—1986, 1987 and 1988. Look for these and you'll be well on your way to a complete collection of the best in holiday romance.

Plus, as an added bonus, you can receive a FREE keepsake Christmas ornament. Just collect four proofs of purchase from any November or December 1992 Harlequin or Silhouette series novels, or from any Harlequin or Silhouette Christmas collection, and receive a beautiful dated brass Christmas candle ornament.

Mail this certificate along with four (4) proof-of-purchase coupons, plus $1.50 postage and handling (check or money order—do not send cash), payable to Silhouette Books, to: **In the U.S.:** P.O. Box 9057, Buffalo, NY 14269-9057; **In Canada:** P.O. Box 622, Fort Erie, Ontario, L2A 5X3.

ONE PROOF OF PURCHASE	Name: _____ _____ Address: _____ _____ City: _____ State/Province: _____ Zip/Postal Code: _____

SX92POP

093 KAG